The Lincoln Reporter

ELVIS IS BACK, AND HE'S IN THE SIXTH GRADE!

by Annie Frootzmacher

Eldon Grant looks like an ordinary sixth-grader. But this reporter recently interviewed Mr. Grant and learned the startling details. Not only does he have a name that's similar to Elvis Presley's, Eldon plays guitar and loves to rock—just like the king of rock and roll. In fact, Eldon's parents fell in love to Presley's music, and his mother still listens to the King almost daily.

Coincidence, you say? Perhaps. But what about this: Eldon was born on August 16th. The same day that Elvis died!

When I asked Eldon about all these facts, his comment was this:

"It's funny. But sometimes I actually think I am Elvis. It's like my destiny or something."

Eldon performs this week at the sixth-grade talent show. There's no doubt in this reporter's mind that after you hear him you'll believe that Lincoln's own Eldon Grant is Elvis!!!!!

Skylark Books you will enjoy
Ask your bookseller for the books you have missed

ELVIS IS BACK, AND HE'S IN THE SIXTH GRADE!

Stephen Mooser

A SKYLARK BOOK®

NEW YORK · TORONTO · LONDON · SYDNEY · AUCKLAND

RL4.0, 008–012

ELVIS IS BACK, AND HE'S IN THE SIXTH GRADE!

A Skylark Book / October 1994

Skylark Books is a registered trademark of Bantam Books, a division of Bantam Doubleday Dell Publishing Group, Inc. Registered in U.S. Patent and Trademark Office and elsewhere.

ISBN 0-553-48177-0

Published simultaneously in the United States and Canada

Bantam Books are published by Bantam Books, a division of Bantam Doubleday Dell Publishing Group, Inc. Its trademark, consisting of the words "Bantam Books" and the portrayal of a rooster, is Registered in U.S. Patent and Trademark Office and in other countries. Marca Registrada. Bantam Books, 1540 Broadway, New York, New York 10036.

PRINTED IN THE UNITED STATES OF AMERICA

OPM   10 9 8 7 6 5 4 3

For the Wheelers, Hook, Anne, Jesse,
Daniel, and Bik

CONTENTS

1

ZAP!

Eldon Grant looked down at his guitar and moaned. His Elvis imitation for the talent show was going to be a disaster. What if he peed in his pants in front of the whole school? Or worse, what if he froze up and had to be carried offstage like a department store dummy? Eldon shifted the retainer around in his mouth and tried to imagine the great Elvis Presley freezing up onstage or peeing in his pants. It seemed most unlikely.

He pulled the curtain back a few inches and peered out into the school auditorium. Nearly every seat was filled with students. Nearly every space along the walls was filled with teachers, and nearly all of them were looking for signs of trouble.

As usual there were plenty. Lenny DeMuro was climbing over his seat, trying to get at Danny Washington. Jeremy Norton was manufacturing paper airplanes, and Angela Barnes was throwing them as fast as they came off the assembly line. Everyone else was either looking bored or poking their neighbor. It smelled like pizza from the cafeteria and sounded like the national yelling championships.

Eldon's worst nightmare, Henry Botkins, was sitting in the front row. From the red cap turned backwards on his big round head, down to the high-top sneakers stuck out into the aisle waiting to trip someone, Henry was a disaster waiting to happen. Henry couldn't be sitting in a worse place either, Eldon thought. It was the same seat he'd been in last year when he'd water-ballooned Eldon during the fifth-grade talent show.

"Eldon Grant!" Annie Frootzmacher strutted across the school stage. "Orange sneakers, baggy checkered pants, a T-shirt with a teddy bear on the front?" She shook her head. "What kind of Elvis costume is that?"

Eldon squinted at Annie. There was a galaxy of tiny plastic stars in her frizzy hair, a fake snake tattoo on her cheek, and a pair of polka-dotted sneakers on her feet. "You look a little weird yourself, you know."

"Weird?" said Annie, putting a finger to her cheek. "Me?"

"I thought we were friends," Eldon moaned. "Geez, how could you have done this to me?"

"Done what?"

Eldon glared at her. What had Annie done? Oh, only run a headline in the school paper announcing that Eldon was going to be the star of the talent show. The front page of last week's *Lincoln Reporter* had announced in giant letters: ELVIS IS BACK, AND HE'S IN THE SIXTH GRADE!

Under the headline Annie had gone on to claim that there were all these weird connections between Eldon and Elvis. She'd even quoted Eldon as saying he sometimes felt like the real Elvis.

"Ah-choo!" Eldon sneezed his retainer into his hand. He sniffled, and then wiped off the retainer on his shirt. "Geez, Annie, you made such a big deal about the Elvis stuff that I couldn't get out of the show. Now everybody is going to see me make a fool of myself, just like last year."

"You're going to be great," said Annie, patting one of his round cheeks. "Relax."

Eldon shook his head. The noise in the auditorium had risen to a roar, then suddenly the lights dimmed and the Lincoln principal, Mrs. Popper, strode out to the microphone. She held a finger to her tight, thin lips, calling for quiet.

When that didn't work, she whipped out a silver whistle and blew on it till her cheeks turned red and her eyes stuck out like Ping-Pong balls. Her eyes did that a lot. That was why everyone called her Mrs. Popeye.

"QUIET!" she yelled into the microphone.

Stunned, everyone shut up.

"Without further ado," Mrs. Popeye said, "let's give a big Lincoln welcome to our first talent this morning, Eldon Grant!"

Eldon gulped. He wanted some further ado.

"Eldon, get out there!" commanded Annie.

Eldon moaned.

"I said *go!*" said Annie, emphasizing the point with a shove.

"Whoa!" yelled Eldon, tumbling onto the stage. He pitched forward, nose first.

"Whoops!" he cried, catching hold of the microphone stand just before he fell.

"At least I didn't land on my butt," he mumbled, broadcasting his words over the microphone.

The audience hooted and laughed. Eldon looked up just as a wad of paper hit him on the head.

"It's Elvis before he knew how to walk!" yelled Henry from the front row.

"He tripped on his blue suede shoes!" yelled someone else.

"Shhhh!" hissed twenty teachers.

"Go on!" yelled Annie.

Eldon tightened his hold on the microphone stand, then looked down at his guitar. He seemed surprised to see it.

"Sing!" yelled Annie.

The best Eldon could do was let out a pathetic little squeak.

"It's Elvis before he could talk!" yelled Henry.

Now Eldon was certain he would pee in his pants.

Offstage, Mrs. Popper was frantically waving at him with the back of her hand. Eldon squinted in her direction. He couldn't tell if she wanted him to sing or to run off the stage. It really didn't matter either way. He was so scared he couldn't move his mouth or his legs.

The students began to clap. "Sing! Sing! Sing!" they chanted.

Eldon held on to the stand to keep from fainting.

"Elvis! Elvis! Elvis!" cried the crowd, stomping their feet.

"Shhhhh!" went twenty teachers.

Suddenly, from out of the audience, a round red missile came hurtling toward Eldon. He could see it coming, but he was helpless to do anything about it.

Kablam! It slammed into his face and exploded.

"Oooof!" Eldon's retainer went flying into the second row. Water was everywhere, soaking his clothes, dripping from his nose, and drenching the microphone.

Wham! Zap! A jolt of electricity welded his hands to the metal stand. His wavy hair uncrinkled and shot up. His tongue stuck out, and his eyes nearly exploded.

"Wow!" someone yelled.

Eldon looked like a cartoon character with his finger in the socket. A few seconds later, his hands still glued to the stand, he started bouncing wildly about the stage, like a bunny on fast-forward. Desperately he tried to get his hands off the stand. But he couldn't.

"Help him!" cried Angela Barnes. "He's been juiced!"

Every cell in his body was vibrating. Rainbows of color were careening about his skull. Out of control, he tap-danced across the stage, then back again.

Wham! Somehow he hit a chord on the guitar.

Whing! Whang! Zang! Three more notes rattled the

walls of the auditorium. Everyone in the place was on their feet and screaming.

"Cut the power!" someone yelled.

"He's frying!" shouted someone else.

The gym teacher ran to call an ambulance. Angela Barnes shielded her eyes. Henry Botkins was quiet for once, his mouth wide open.

Twing! Another note.

Eldon's eyebrows were at attention. Sparks were flying from his hair. Then, suddenly, somehow, his hands snapped open and the microphone clattered to the floor.

"He's free!" yelled Annie.

The crowd was in a frenzy, waving their arms, screaming, as if somehow they'd been electrified too. There had been a lot of talent shows at Lincoln over the years, featuring some pretty good acts. But nobody had seen anything like the performance Eldon had just delivered.

For a moment or two Eldon didn't move. He stood rooted to the floor, legs spread, fighting to catch his breath. Then he raised his lip and sneered, as if he'd been doing it his whole life.

They hadn't seen anything yet.

2

THE KING

 *Blam!* In a single motion Eldon raised his guitar, then dropped it between his legs, nearly doing the splits.

Wham! The opening note of "Hound Dog" shook the room.

"You ain't nothing but a hound dog!" shouted Eldon.

Shaking his hips, he twisted up to the edge of the stage and dropped to his knees.

"You ain't never caught a rabbit and you ain't no friend of mine!" *Wham-a-da-whamma-da-wham!*

Wow! Eldon was as surprised as anyone at what was happening. The jolt of juice had changed something inside him, but he wasn't quite sure yet what it was.

The audience stood in stunned silence, their mouths wide open.

Bam!

Eldon was suddenly back on his feet. He planted one leg squarely on the stage and started shaking the other as he screamed out "Hound Dog."

The voice and the moves kept on coming. The shock of electricity had done more than just tingle his brain. He was rolling through "Hound Dog" like a man possessed.

It must have been a minute or two till Angela Barnes finally broke the stunned silence of the crowd.

"Ellll———vis!" she screamed, her hands alongside her head. "It's him!"

Then all at once everyone was going crazy, jumping up and down, waving their arms, and screaming for Elvis.

Even Mrs. Popeye started tapping her toes. Two teachers, Mr. Keefe and Mrs. Blaney, began dancing in the aisle.

So many arms were waving over so many heads that from the stage Eldon thought he was looking out at a sea of snakes.

"It's the King!" cried Angela Barnes.

For the moment at least, it was.

Eldon shook and strummed and sang and strutted

like he owned the world. Finally, his face streaming with sweat, he twisted to the front of the stage, pointed his guitar out at the crowd, and wrapped up the song.

Wow!

Eldon thrust the guitar over his head.

The auditorium exploded with cheers and applause.

Eldon waved his guitar and drank in the glory.

"Elvis!" chanted the crowd. A flashbulb exploded, then another.

"Thank you, folks," said Eldon. He blew the audience a kiss, then checked his pants.

They were dry.

3

MISS LILLY

There was no point in continuing the talent show. No one could follow Eldon. Not Iris Meehan singing the theme from *The Brady Bunch*. Not Stevie Sprague playing "Chopsticks." And certainly not Lucy Wheeler's silly animal imitations.

"Off to lunch!" shouted Mrs. Popper, her eyes bugging out.

The students tumbled out of the auditorium, talking excitedly about what they'd just seen.

Smiling and sweaty, Eldon swaggered offstage and into Annie Frootzmacher's arms.

"I knew you could do it!" she said. She shook her head, unleashing a snowstorm of tiny plastic stars. "Wow!"

"It weren't nothing, ma'm," said Eldon. He winked.

"Weren't nothing? Ma'm?" said Annie. She grinned. "When did you ever pick up that Southern accent?"

"Ma'm, I don't rightly know," he said. "Seems kinda natural though, don't it?"

Just then someone grabbed Eldon's hand. When he looked down, his eyes met those of a freckle-faced fourth-grader named Tammy Wilson.

"I think this is yours," she said, pressing Eldon's pink retainer into his palm. She blushed. "It hit me when you spit it out."

"Little lady, I'm right sorry about that," said Eldon.

"Don't be sorry. I felt honored," said Tammy. She squeezed his hand and gave him a dreamy look. "I'll hold your retainer anytime."

Eldon winked.

"Ah-hem!" said Annie, clearing her throat. "Shouldn't you be running along to lunch?" She pulled Tammy's hand away. "Your pizza is getting cold."

"Oh," said Tammy.

"Go!" said Annie, giving her a push.

Tammy gave Eldon a little wave, then ran off, giggling.

"Of all the nerve," said Annie.

"I thought it was nice," said Eldon. "I'm not used to being noticed around here."

Bang! The door at the side of the stage flew open and two men in white uniforms burst through, carrying a stretcher.

"Where's the kid that got juiced?" asked one of them, a bald man with floppy bulldog cheeks. He put the stretcher on the floor.

"Did he already croak?" asked the other man, scratching himself in the ribs.

"No, he didn't croak," said Annie. "He's right here." She pointed at Eldon with her thumb.

"I barely got shocked," said Eldon. "Believe me, sir. I ain't the least bit hurt."

"We'll let the doctor decide that," said the man. He pointed at the stretcher. "Lie down and we'll take you to the hospital."

"I told you I'm fine," said Eldon.

"Better do as he says," said Mrs. Popper, rushing backstage. "That was quite a jolt you got."

"Must I, ma'm?" said Eldon, squinting up at his principal.

"School policy," said Mrs. Popper. "I'm sure these gentlemen will take good care of you."

Eldon sighed, handed Annie the guitar, and got down on the stretcher.

"I feel silly," he said as he was carried out the door and into the parking lot. An ambulance, its lights flashing, was waiting. Like a pizza being placed in an oven, Eldon was lifted into the rear of the vehicle. Then the ambulance pulled away, siren screaming.

Eldon stared up at the ceiling as they raced through the streets of downtown Lincoln. The truth was, he'd never felt better in his life. Sure, it had felt weird when he'd first been shocked, but seeing all those kids' faces and hearing them scream his name over and over again had cured that in a hurry. Eldon had never had so much attention in his life.

When they arrived at Lincoln General Hospital a few minutes later, the attendants flung open the ambulance doors. Then they placed Eldon and the stretcher on a gurney and wheeled him into the emergency room.

A nurse escorted him to a chair and then plunked a clipboard with forms attached down in front of Eldon. "Fill these out, Elvis," she said, giving him a big wink.

As Eldon read over the papers, an old lady looked over his shoulder.

Eldon glanced up. The woman had white stringy hair, and her skin was even whiter than her hair. Her lips were dry and cracked. Judging by the slippers on her feet and her worn purple robe, she'd been brought to the emergency room in a hurry.

The woman leaned closer, and Eldon glanced nervously around the room. What does she want from me? he wondered. Everything in the place was made of either stainless steel or plastic. The smell of medicine and musty old magazines filled the heavy air. Except for the nurse behind the desk, Eldon and the old woman were the only people in the waiting area.

I hate hospitals, Eldon thought with a shiver. He went back to filling out the form.

"I can't stand hospitals either," said the old woman suddenly. "Especially the emergency room. You never know what kind of horrible thing might come rolling through the door."

Eldon looked at the woman with surprise. It was as if she'd just read his mind.

It's what everybody who comes to a hospital thinks, Eldon told himself. He started writing faster, hoping to chase away his creepy feelings.

"You know, you have very interesting handwriting," said the woman in her raspy voice. She leaned over Eldon's shoulder. "It says a lot about you."

I wish she would leave me alone, thought Eldon, not looking up.

"It says you're going to be famous, and rich too."

"Yeah, right," Eldon mumbled, and shook his head.

"Let me see your hand," said the woman.

"Huh?" Eldon squinted at her.

"Let me read your palm," she said. "I'll tell you your life."

If I let her do it, Eldon thought, maybe she'll just leave me alone. He held out his palm.

"I've been reading palms for sixty years," the woman said. "Perhaps you've heard of me: Lilly Springwater. Most people just call me Miss Lilly."

Eldon looked around again. Where were the doctors? Miss Lilly was a nut case if he'd ever seen one. No wonder she was at the hospital.

"I see lots of happiness here," she said, tracing a line on Eldon's palm with her finger. "You like music, don't you?"

Eldon nodded.

"Capricorns like music," said Miss Lilly. She put a finger to her forehead and thought. "You were born in January. The eighth to be exact."

Eldon rolled his eyes. "August sixteenth."

Miss Lilly smiled. "No, I'm quite sure of the date."

"Yeah, well so am I," said Eldon.

"Why isn't this interesting. You and your cousin are worm diggers."

18

"What?" said Eldon. He laughed.

"You spend your summers digging up worms, then fishing in the lake," said Miss Lilly.

"I hate worms—fish, too," said Eldon.

"I see terrible fear," Miss Lilly went on. "You're crouched in the basement. There's a tornado outside." She moaned. "Oh, my. The noise is terrible."

"Lincoln doesn't have tornadoes and my house doesn't have a basement," said Eldon. He tried to yank away his hand, but Miss Lilly wouldn't let him go.

"Not so fast, young man," said Miss Lilly. Her blue eyes glowed softly, as if lit from behind. "There's more . . . Uh! I see tragedy. You've let your fame and your money get to your head. And just look at what you've done to your body. My, all that junk food!"

Eldon rolled his eyes. What was she talking about?

Suddenly Miss Lilly gasped and let go of Eldon's hand.

"This is awful."

"What do you mean?"

"Your future," she said. She put a hand to her tiny mouth. "I'm sorry. I've said too much already."

Eldon squinted into the old woman's shimmering blue eyes. "Not that I believe you, but . . ."

"Listen, and listen carefully," she interrupted, clapping her hands onto Eldon's cheeks. "Do not doubt my words. You're in terrible danger!"

"I am?" said Eldon. He gulped and looked around.

Miss Lilly's face was whiter than chalk. She dropped her hands into her lap and peered into Eldon's eyes. "Someone's trying to kill you!"

Eldon gasped. "Lady, please. You're scaring me."

"You ought to be scared," she said. She chewed on her lip. "Oh, if only I could do something."

"Whoa. Wait a minute," said Eldon.

Miss Lilly got to her feet. Eldon was surprised at how short she was. "Nothing good can come of this," she said.

"Come of what?"

The old woman threw back her head and groaned, as if she'd been socked in the stomach. Then, without another word, she turned and shuffled out the door in her bathrobe and slippers.

"Hey! Just wait a darn minute here!" said Eldon, getting to his feet. "Don't just up and leave me like this!"

The nurse raised her head. "Are you finished?" she asked.

Eldon looked down at the form, then back up at the nurse. "Who was that woman?"

"Why Miss Lilly, of course. Haven't you heard of her, Mr. Grant?"

"Hey, how did you know my name?" asked Eldon. "I didn't tell anyone."

"Miss Lilly told me you were coming," said the nurse. "Don't you know? She predicts the future. Quite accurately, too."

4

GRITS

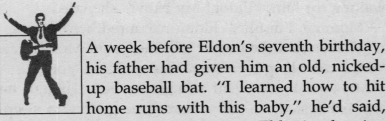 A week before Eldon's seventh birthday, his father had given him an old, nicked-up baseball bat. "I learned how to hit home runs with this baby," he'd said, placing his big, warm hands over Eldon's, showing him how to grip the bat. "Tomorrow, first thing, I'm going to show you how to hit homers too, just like my daddy taught me."

"I'm going to be the next Babe Ruth," Eldon vowed.

"You bet, son," his father said, smiling proudly.

Then Mr. Grant went off to work and never came back. Just three blocks away, his car was hit by another car, and he was killed instantly.

Eldon was thinking about his father as the nurse ushered him into a small examination room. His father had been brought to this same hospital five years ago. On that day his future had ended. If Miss Lilly was right, was Eldon's life almost over too?

Eldon sat shivering in his white gown as he waited for the doctor. Finally a small man with dark hair and glasses entered and checked Eldon from head to toe.

"You're in perfect health," he pronounced.

Relieved, Eldon got dressed and went back out to the waiting area. His mother was there, anxiously waiting for him. "Eldon! My baby!" she cried.

"Momma, I'm fine," Eldon reassured her.

"That's what the doctor told me," said Mrs. Grant. "But I can't help worrying. You're all I've got."

At home Eldon went straight to bed. Though he was exhausted, he had a hard time getting to sleep. He couldn't stop thinking about the fortune-teller's predictions, nor could he forget how great it had felt to be onstage. Everyone in the school had been looking at him. Everyone in the school had loved him.

In the morning his mother gave him a bowl of his favorite cereal, Sugar Stars.

"Don't we have any grits?" he asked, pushing the bowl away.

"Grits?" said Mrs. Grant, looking up from her own

bowl of Sugar Stars. "People in the South eat grits. I wouldn't even know how to make them."

"Grits ain't much but a mess of ground, cooked corn," said Eldon, surprising himself. He'd never eaten grits before, much less craved them. "They're delicious."

"Eldon, are you sure you're all right?" said Mrs. Grant.

"Momma, I told you last night, there ain't nothing wrong with me," said Eldon.

Mrs. Grant sighed. "You just don't seem yourself," she said. "And where did you pick up that Southern accent?"

"I don't rightly know," said Eldon. "But ever since I got that shock . . ." He considered telling her about Miss Lilly and her prediction, then thought better of it. His mom would only worry. He grinned. "You should have seen me at that talent show, Momma. I swear, I sounded just like Elvis. The other kids went crazy. They loved it."

"I wish I'd been there," said Mrs. Grant. She sighed and lowered her eyes. "You know how I feel about the king of rock and roll."

"I know, Momma," Eldon said solemnly. His parents had owned all of Elvis's records and gone to many of his concerts. In fact, the night before Mr. Grant died, they'd spent hours dancing slowly to the music of their favorite song, "Can't Help Falling in Love."

"Guess what, Momma? As soon as I get rich I'm going to buy you a big ol' Cadillac, a pink one?"

"A Cadillac?" said Mrs. Grant, confused.

"The biggest one they got," said Eldon. He stood up and grabbed a muffin. "I'll just have this for breakfast. We can start with the grits tomorrow morning."

Mrs. Grant shook her head. "Take care of yourself. Please."

"Don't worry about me, Momma," he said. "I'm just fine. Actually I'm more than fine—I'm a superstar now."

Then Eldon swaggered out the door in his teddy bear T-shirt, baggy checkered pants, and orange sneakers.

5

IT'S A DEAL

 Eldon usually slid into school unnoticed. Aside from Annie he had no friends. He thought most kids didn't like him.

The truth was that most kids didn't know he existed.

But that was before.

"Hey. You were good yesterday," said Angela Barnes, catching up to him in the hallway that morning.

Eldon looked over and smiled. Angela had big dark eyes and long hair cascading over her shoulders. He blushed.

"You sounded just like Elvis, really," said Angela. "How long have you been practicing?"

"I didn't practice at all," said Eldon in his Southern accent. "It just kind of came on natural like."

Angela chewed on her lip and studied Eldon's teddy bear T-shirt as they walked. "I like the way you dress," she said.

Eldon looked down at his shirt. He'd probably worn it a thousand times. Henry Botkins was always making jokes about it.

"Where did you get that shirt?" asked Angela. They had stopped outside the journalism room.

"K mart, I think," said Eldon.

"I'm going to get one," said Angela. "It's so cool."

Eldon looked down at his shirt again. By the time he looked up, Angela was gone, hurrying to her first class.

"Hey, hound dog!" yelled Josh Hodgkins, waving as he hurried by. "You were great!"

Eldon gave Josh a little half wave in return. "Thank you, son. But it weren't nothing, really."

A clump of third-graders came by, pointed at Eldon, and then ran off, giggling.

He waved after them. "Weren't nothing," he repeated, liking the way it sounded.

The journalism room was empty except for Annie, who was busy loading the latest issue of *The Lincoln Reporter* onto a cart.

The headline in the paper read: MONSTERS FOUND IN SCHOOL BASEMENT!

Eldon shook his head. "This is the kind of fake headline you'd see in a paper like *The National Whisper*," he said.

"It's not fake," said Annie. "The janitors found some old monster costumes down there last week. All I'm doing is reporting the news."

"Just like you reported I was Elvis," said Eldon.

"Hey, I did you a favor," said Annie. "In case you haven't noticed, everyone's talking about you today. How did you manage to do such a good impression of Elvis anyway?"

Eldon shrugged. "I don't know. I was about to run offstage when I got that shock. And after that . . . I don't know why or how, but when I started to sing and play guitar, I felt like a real performer."

"You sounded like one, too," Annie said, looking as surprised as Eldon felt. "I hate to say it, but getting electrocuted was one of the best things that's ever happened to you. I've been thinking—"

"Is this another one of your schemes?" Eldon interrupted.

"This is no scheme," said Annie, putting a hand on Eldon's shoulder. "This is the real thing. I have an idea. Everyone knows that Elvis impersonators are big business in this country."

"Elvis impersonators?" Eldon interrupted.

"They're everywhere," said Annie. "They sing in nightclubs, at fairs, in concerts, on TV. Haven't you ever seen one?"

Eldon shrugged. "Yeah, maybe. So?"

"Well, there's going to be an impersonator show at the mall in a few weeks. I'm thinking of signing you up."

"I don't know about that," said Eldon.

"Know about it," said Annie. "That is if you want to be rich and famous."

Eldon wrinkled his brow. The old woman had predicted he'd be rich and famous. But she was a crazy old bat. "I'm not an Elvis impersonator," he told Annie.

Annie grinned. "I'm going to be your Colonel Tom Parker."

"My who?"

"Parker was Elvis's manager," said Annie. "He set up jobs for Elvis, just like I'm doing for you."

Eldon gave her a skeptical look.

"Trust me," Annie continued. "Put your future in my hands and you won't be sorry. I'll get you concerts, promotional appearances, endorsements, everything. All you have to do is show up and get famous. Come on. You can't lose."

Eldon chewed on his lip and thought. Annie was

always coming up with crazy ideas, and this one might be the craziest yet. But it had been fun performing yesterday and he could probably manage to sing and dance like that again. What did he have to lose? If Annie was right and he did become rich and famous, then he could ride around in a limousine and buy a big house. And he'd probably never have to worry again about sitting alone in the cafeteria or being picked for a team in gym class. He couldn't just walk away from a possibility like this.

Eldon offered his hand to Annie. "I reckon it's a deal."

After Annie went off to deliver the school newspapers, Eldon went into the bathroom. Standing before the mirror, he wet his hair and combed it back into a ducktail. Then he rolled up the sleeves on his teddy bear T-shirt and flexed his muscles.

Yes, sir, he thought, becoming a famous Elvis impersonator would suit me just fine.

Eldon drifted back into the hallway and spent his morning classes dreaming about his new life.

The first thing he'd do was buy a new house. There would be a swimming pool, of course, and a video arcade and a gym and a movie theater. Lots of bedrooms, all with their own bathrooms for when his friends came over. He'd have lots of friends.

They'll be amazed at all my stuff, he thought, staring out the window while Mrs. Hanson droned on about the French Revolution. But what will amaze them most is that the money and fame didn't go to my head.

"Mr. Grant!" came the voice of Mrs. Hanson. "I'm asking you a question."

"Huh?" said Eldon, squinting.

"Who was the king?"

"Elvis, of course," said Eldon, raising his fist.

Everyone laughed. Everyone but Mrs. Hanson.

"I wasn't talking about the king of rock and roll," said Mrs. Hanson. She was wearing a tight blue suit and a little white bow tie. "I was asking about the king of France during the revolution."

"Sorry, ma'm," said Eldon.

"Well, who was it?"

Eldon shook his head.

"Louis the Sixteenth," she said.

"Oh." Eldon winced.

Mrs. Hanson smiled. "That was a very good imitation you did yesterday," she said. "It took me back."

Lisa Treadway leaned across the aisle and patted Eldon's shoulder.

"What?" whispered Eldon, turning around.

Lisa giggled.

Everyone was looking at Eldon. He raised his lip and gave everyone the famous Elvis sneer. There was a long silence. Mrs. Hanson blushed and straightened her little bow tie. "Well, class, we'd better move along."

6

ON TOUR

Annie kept Eldon busy for the next three days.

His first job as an Elvis impersonator was an appearance on Wednesday at the Record Shack. Unfortunately, it looked like fame wasn't going to happen overnight. Only one person showed up for the autographing—Tammy Wilson.

"Where's everyone else?" asked Eldon, signing his fifteenth autograph for Tammy. "Don't they know the King's in town?"

"I don't think so," said Tammy, staring dreamily into Eldon's eyes. "The only reason I'm here is because I've been following you around."

Eldon whirled around to face Annie. "Didn't you put up any signs?" he demanded.

"Of course," said Annie. "But I've been so busy lining up other events, I didn't get as many up as I hoped."

Eldon growled. "Don't let it happen again."

"Yes, sir," said Annie. "You're the boss."

Eldon slicked back his hair with his hand, raised an eyebrow, and gave Annie his best Elvis sneer. "I ain't the boss, sweet pea. I am the King."

"You know it," said Tammy. She grabbed Eldon's hand and gave it a squeeze. "You're the greatest rock and roller of all time!"

Annie rolled her eyes. Eldon slicked back his hair one more time and sneered.

On Thursday afternoon Annie had lined up another job for Eldon: speaking to the old people at the Sunshine Nursing Home. Tammy watched through the window. Everyone else slept through the talk.

On Friday Eldon was due at the Food Giant supermarket. As part of his costume he wore a special belt that had belonged to his father. Artist of the Year was written across the giant gold belt buckle. It was just like the belts Elvis Presley had worn in concert.

Eldon and Annie got to the Food Giant a few minutes after four on Friday afternoon.

"Why do you think a supermarket would want Elvis hanging around?" asked Eldon.

"To bring in customers," said Annie, leading Eldon into the market. "Mr. Crane is a businessman. He has promotions like this all the time."

The market was filled with shoppers. The clattering of carts, the chattering of people, and the smell of baked bread all mingled under the glow of the Food Giant's fluorescent ceiling.

"Excuse me," said Annie, approaching one of the checkout clerks. "I'm looking for Mr. Crane. Elvis Presley is here."

The clerk, a sour-faced man wearing a paper Food Giant crown proclaiming him the King of Good Service, looked past Annie and searched the store. "Elvis Presley! Where?"

Annie pointed her thumb at Eldon. Eldon raised the corner of his lip and sneered. "Love me tender, love me true," he crooned in a deep, Elvis voice.

The clerk laughed and called to his friend at the next register. "Do you know where Mr. Crane is? Elvis Presley is here to see him."

The other checkout clerk kept bagging groceries and never looked up. "It's four o'clock. He's probably polishing tomatoes."

"Thanks," said Annie, and she and Eldon headed for the produce department.

"Are you sure he's expecting us?" asked Eldon.

"Don't worry," Annie assured him. "Mr. Crane knows you're coming. He knows everything that goes on here."

Eldon had to agree. Mr. Crane watched over his store like a fussy mother. Day or night you could catch him prowling the aisles, making sure every can was perfect, every box was in its place, and every apple was polished.

Sure enough, they found him in the produce department, topping off a pyramid of tomatoes.

"Mr. Crane?" said Annie.

Mr. Crane turned around, adjusted his bow tie, and gave her a sugary smile. "Yes, young lady. How may I serve you?"

"I'm Annie Frootzmacher," she said, extending her hand. "I talked to you on the phone a few days ago. Remember?"

"Of course I remember," said Mr. Crane. His thin hair was parted down the middle and greased to his skull. "We've had signs up for the last two days advertising the big event." He smiled at Eldon. "We're expecting quite a crowd."

"See? What did I tell you," said Annie.

"It's about time," said Eldon. He turned to Mr. Crane. "So, what do you want me to do? Sign autographs? Pose for pictures? Wiggle my hips and make all the ladies scream?"

"Wiggle your hips?" Mr. Crane blushed, then quickly returned to building his tomato pyramid. "Whatever you normally do at these things is fine with me."

"Well, I suppose I could sing, but I didn't bring my guitar," said Eldon.

Mr. Crane looked at his watch. "We've got nearly half an hour. I'll hunt up a guitar. Miss Hays in the meat department has your costume."

"Costume?" said Eldon.

"What costume?" said Annie.

"Crispy, crunchy, salty too. Twisty, turny, through and through," Mr. Crane sang. "Why, the Mr. Pretzel costume, of course."

"Mr. Pretzel?" echoed Annie.

"The man on the bag of the world's crunchiest pretzels. The man who sings the Mr. Pretzel song on TV," said Mr. Crane.

Eldon narrowed his eyes. "Annie."

"You're not Mr. Pretzel?" asked Mr. Crane.

"He's Elvis Presley, the rock and roll singer," said Annie.

39

"Not Mr. Pretzel?" repeated Mr. Crane.

"Elvis Presley," repeated Annie.

"But isn't he dead?" asked Mr. Crane. He looked confused.

Eldon shook his head. "Come on, Annie. Let's go."

"Whoa, not so fast," said Mr. Crane. He grabbed Eldon by the arm. "I have a promotion here in half an hour. I've got the costume and everything. I was counting on you."

Annie held out her hands. "Gosh, Eldon, I don't see where you have a choice."

"Can you learn the Mr. Pretzel song?" asked Mr. Crane hopefully. He let go of Eldon and clapped his hands as he sang, "Crispy, crunchy, salty, too. Twisty—"

"Stop!" said Eldon, raising his hand. "Don't sing another word. You'll have your Mr. Pretzel."

Mr. Crane grinned. "Thank goodness."

Eldon pointed to Annie. "Here he is. This little lady here knows the song and everything."

"Really?" said Mr. Crane.

"She's in love with Mr. Pretzel," Eldon went on. "She even started his fan club."

"I did nothing of the sort!" said Annie. She whipped out an arm, hoping to catch Eldon in the ribs. But he jumped aside and her arm slammed into the pyramid of tomatoes instead. "Whoops!"

"My display!" shrieked Mr. Crane. He reached out desperately, but it was too late. The tomatoes came tumbling down.

Annie and Eldon watched in horror as the tomato avalanche poured past them and headed for the milk case.

"Help!" yelled Mr. Crane, scrambling after his runaway produce. "Help! Help!"

Annie's face was as red as the tomatoes. "Sorry, Eldon," she muttered. She bent down, trying to scoop up the fruit.

"Take it away, sweet pea," said Eldon, tiptoeing through the mess. "See you later."

Mr. Crane looked at Eldon. Then he turned to Annie. "You've got to help me out. There are going to be a hundred people here in half an hour looking for Mr. Pretzel."

"But . . ." said Annie.

"You just have to help me." Mr. Crane fell onto his knees and clasped his hands together in prayer. "I can't let my customers down. I can't."

"Please don't beg," said Annie. "You're making me feel guilty."

"Oh, thank you, thank you," said Mr. Crane, scrambling to his feet. "You don't know what this means to me."

"But . . . but . . ." sputtered Annie.

Mr. Crane raised his hand. "Don't move. I'll be right back with the costume."

7

THE NATIONAL WHISPER

"Whoa!" yelled Eldon on Saturday morning when he spotted the latest edition of *The National Whisper* at the West End Drug Store. The headline filled nearly half the page, and the picture of him holding a guitar filled the rest.

ELVIS IS BACK!
AND HE'S IN THE SIXTH GRADE!

"Oh my." Eldon gasped. "*The National Whisper* is sold all over the country!" He shook his head. Yesterday, after the disaster at the Food Giant, Eldon had given up on Annie and her claims that she could make him famous. Now here he was on the cover of a national newspaper. How had she done it?

The story filled the entire second page. It was all about Eldon's performance and how much he had sounded like the real Elvis.

The reporter had also interviewed the president of the Elvis Society.

"After seeing the photos and watching the video-tape, I believe Eldon Grant is Elvis," said Mrs. Mary Ann Zubeck. "It makes perfect sense to me that Elvis would choose to return to earth as a boy. Why would he want to come back as an adult? He was messed up on drugs and alcohol and his ego. He blew it and he knew it. I do believe he plans to do it right this time."

Eldon's eyes dropped down to the bottom of the article. There was a grainy picture there. Eldon gasped. It was Miss Lilly!

"The boy is Elvis," she was quoted as saying. "There's no doubt in my mind. But I'm afraid things won't be any different this time. The boy is doomed, just like the man. It's his destiny."

Eldon's hands were shaking so badly he couldn't hold the paper steady.

Blam! Someone slapped him on the back. "Yikes!" he screamed, nearly leaping into the next aisle.

"I thought I saw you come in here. What do you think?"

Eldon caught his breath, and turned. Annie grinned. She was wearing a Mr. Pretzel T-shirt, featuring the salty, crunchy snack himself wearing a top hat and holding a cane. "Am I an expert on publicity or what!"

"Why didn't you tell me about this?" said Eldon, slapping the paper with the back of his hand.

"I wanted it to be a surprise," said Annie. "Aren't you excited! We just went national!"

"Now go national with this: Eldon Quits Being Elvis!" he said.

"What are you talking about?" said Annie.

"Didn't you read this story?" said Eldon. "Miss Lilly says I'm doomed. Money and fame ain't worth dying for, no sir."

Annie rolled her eyes. "Come on, Eldon. Do you really believe the garbage they put in the *Whisper*?"

"I don't know what to believe," said Eldon. "But that woman gives me the creeps."

"You're just a little shaky from that shock, that's all." Annie put her hands on Eldon's shoulders and looked him in the eye. "You can't quit now. Do you want to be little wimpy Eldon Grant for the rest of your life?"

"No. But at least wimpy Eldon might have the rest of a life." He moaned. "I don't know, Annie. Sometimes being Elvis is fun. But there are times when I just want to be myself again. I feel so . . . different."

"What do you mean?" Annie asked. "You look the same to me."

Eldon shook his head. "Something happened to me when I got that shock. This morning at breakfast I complained about my grits. Then I promised Momma I'd buy her a pink Cadillac." Eldon looked at Annie. "Can you believe that? Now where would I get a fool idea like that?"

Annie fished a thin blue book from the pocket of her jeans. *Elvis, His Life and Times*, it said on the cover.

"Have you been reading this book?"

Eldon shook his head.

"Then how'd you know about that Cadillac?"

"What Cadillac?"

"The pink one Elvis bought for his mother the second he got rich and famous."

Eldon just stared at her. How had he known about the pink car? Maybe it was true. Maybe Miss Lilly and Mary Ann Zubeck were right. Somehow he— Eldon Grant, an ordinary sixth-grader—had actually become the king of rock and roll.

8

THE CENTER OF ATTENTION

 After *The National Whisper* appeared on newsstands, Eldon's phone rang all weekend.

"No, I'm not Elvis," he told some of the callers.

"Yes, ma'm, I am," he said to others.

He couldn't make up his mind.

On Monday before school he had one bowl of grits, then a bowl of Sugar Stars.

"I worry about you," said Mrs. Grant. "Your eyes are red all the time, and your skin is kind of yellow. Are you all right?"

Eldon stood up, sighed, and grabbed his backpack. "I'm just tired, Momma. Being Elvis is hard work. Please, don't worry none."

47

"I can't help it," said Mrs. Grant. "You're all I've got, you know."

Eldon patted his mother on the cheek. "Cheer up, Momma. Come on now, be my little teddy bear."

Mrs. Grant bit her lip. " 'Teddy Bear,' that was one of your father's favorite Elvis songs. He called me teddy bear, too."

Eldon paused at the door and looked back at his mother. She was staring off somewhere, remembering. Eldon sighed. He wished he could bring back his dad. A pink Cadillac would be nice, but it wasn't what she really needed.

It was a warm spring day. Trees were sprouting leaves, lawns were turning green, and everything smelled fresh and new. Eldon took in a deep breath, then started for school, whistling the tune of "Heartbreak Hotel."

Before he'd gone half a block, an old white Cadillac with two women inside rolled up and slowed to a crawl.

"Ell-vis!" yelled the big, bushy-haired lady leaning out the window. "Yoo-hoo!"

Eldon squinted.

The woman was holding a camera.

"Yoo! Hoo!"

Blam! A flashbulb exploded. Eldon shielded his eyes.

"Welcome back, Elvis!" yelled the woman.

Eldon raised a hand and started walking faster. The Cadillac sped up.

"Can I get an autograph?" asked the woman. She had put away the camera and was holding out a pad of paper and a pencil. "Yoo-hoo! Elvis!"

Eldon shook his head. "Ma'm, you got the wrong guy!"

"You can't fool me, Elvis. I seen your picture in the *Whisper*," said the woman. She shook the pad of paper at Eldon. "Puh-leeze! My friend Irene and I drove all night from Texas just to see you."

"You did?" said Eldon. "Just to see me?"

"We left the second we saw the story in the *Whisper*," said the woman. "Puh-leeze?"

Eldon looked around. "Well, all right. I reckon if you came all the way from Texas."

The car stopped and Eldon walked over.

"Sign it, 'To Irene and Annabelle, Love, Elvis Presley,' " said the woman, handing Eldon the pen.

Eldon autographed the pad just the way the woman wanted.

When he handed it back she looked at the autograph closely. Then she put a hand to her cheek and screeched. "It's him all right! The signatures match!"

"What?" said Eldon.

"See for yourself," said Annabelle. She passed a magazine out through the window. Elvis's signature was on the cover. Eldon studied it closely. The lady was right. The signatures were identical.

"When are you going to sing?" asked the woman. She smelled awful, just like someone who'd driven all night from Texas. "We want tickets to the concert."

Eldon looked again at Elvis's autograph, then passed the magazine back. "Ain't that something, though?" he said.

"Elvis, we're your biggest fans," said the woman. She put a hand to her mouth and giggled. "We even celebrate your birthday, every year on January eighth."

Eldon gulped. January eighth! Miss Lilly had said that Eldon was born on that day.

"Just look at us, Irene!" squealed Annabelle, grabbing her cheeks. "We're talking to Elvis!"

Eldon forced a smile and walked away. The ladies in the Cadillac followed him for the rest of the way to school, snapping pictures and blowing him kisses.

Eldon tried his best to ignore them, but he had to admit that all the attention was fun. After all, it wasn't every day that someone drove a thousand miles to get his autograph.

When Eldon reached school he discovered that Annabelle and Irene weren't the only ones who had come out to see him. There were fifty people or more gathered on the sidewalk. Signs bobbed over the crowd. ELVIS WE LOVE YOU! said one. THE KING HAS RETURNED said another. ELVIS FOR PRESIDENT said a third.

Eldon slowed and eyed the crowd. They were women mostly, and older. They hadn't seen him yet. But that was all about to change. Annabelle and Irene had parked the car down the street and were hurrying his way.

"Oooh, Elvis," cried Annabelle. She was wearing sparkly green pants that seemed to glitter as she moved. "Wait up!"

Eldon shuddered, then picked up his pace.

The crowd on the street was making a lot of noise, and half the student body, maybe more, had gathered on the lawn to see the show.

Eldon lowered his head and broke into a jog.

"One little kiss!" screamed Annabelle, thundering his way. "You can't escape me, Elvis!"

Eldon looked nervously over his shoulder just as the crowd swung around as one. "ELVIS!"

"It's him!" someone screamed.

Suddenly they were all coming his way, calling his name, waving autograph books, snapping pictures.

Eldon looked at the onrushing stampede, then back at Annabelle huffing his way. With luck, he could beat the crowd to the school door. All he had to do was clear the bushes at the edge of the front lawn. He took two steps, leapt into the air . . . and caught his shoe on a branch.

"Whoa! Whoops! Ayyyy-uh!" he screamed.

Whomp! Down he went, face first.

The blow knocked the wind out of him.

"Eldon!" It was Annie's voice.

It was a few seconds before he could catch his breath.

"Ooo," he moaned, struggling to his knees. He had a clump of mud on his nose and another on his chin. He brushed them off with the back of his hand and tried to get to his feet. Halfway up, he was met head-on by Annabelle.

"OOOOF!" Down he went again.

In a wink the entire mob was on top of him, like flies on jam.

"Sign my book!"

"Let me touch him!"

"Give me one of your famous juicy kisses!"

Rrrrr-ip! "I've got a piece of his shirt!"

Eldon tried to push them away, but he couldn't. There were too many hands grabbing at him. Too many bodies holding him down. For a moment he thought he was going to be smothered to death.

"Help," he mumbled.

Smmmmm-ack! Some old lady kissed him on the cheek.

Rrrrr-ip! "I got his pants!"

"Hey!" yelled Eldon.

"Sign this!"

Rrrrr-ip! Rrrrr-ip!

Ta-weeet! Suddenly the air was split by the sound of Mrs. Popper's whistle.

"Get off my school grounds or I'll have you arrested!"

Everyone quickly unpiled.

Popeye blew the whistle again, turning her eyes into golf balls.

"Scat!" she yelled, shooing them away.

The mob hastily retreated to the sidewalk. Someone waved a hunk of Eldon's T-shirt. Someone else held up a cuff of his pants. Someone else had his shoe.

As several women whipped out their cameras and began taking pictures of Eldon, he staggered to his feet and shook his head. He wasn't quite sure where he was. He wasn't even quite sure who he was. But when he looked down, he was quite sure of one thing. He didn't want to be who he was *or* where he was—alone on the lawn, clothed only in his purple underwear.

9

LOVE ME TENDER

Mrs. Popper marched up to the mob of Elvis fans and gave them a blast from her whistle.

"You should be ashamed of your-selves!" she shouted, pointing at the nearly naked Eldon Grant. "This is a public school!"

Eldon wrapped his arms around his body. Everyone was staring at him.

"Someone run to the gym and bring Eldon some clothes," said the principal, pointing at the students standing on the steps. "Go!"

A few minutes later Tammy Wilson was back with a pair of oversized sweatpants and a Lincoln Junior High T-shirt with the school mascot, Abe Lincoln, on the front.

"Here," said Tammy, blushing.

Eldon was blushing, too. In fact, he'd been blushing steadily for the last ten minutes. He quickly pulled on the clothes. The drawstring was missing from the pants so he had to hold them up with his hand.

Mrs. Popper brought him his missing shoe and led him across the lawn. When they reached the steps she put her hands on her hips and glared at the students.

"What are you doing here? School's on! Move it!"

The students muttered to themselves and headed into the school. To Eldon's surprise, not a single one was laughing at him. Eldon Grant in his underwear was funny, Eldon realized. But *Elvis Presley* in his underwear was something else.

Most of the kids at Lincoln hadn't made up their minds about who he was. But between the sixth-grade talent show, the story in *The National Whisper*, and the mob of fans, he had everyone wondering.

Annie was waiting at the top of the steps. She was wearing a white T-shirt with the sleeves rolled up. A tattoo of an eagle with a lightning bolt in its mouth decorated her arm.

"Are you okay?" she asked, falling in step alongside as they walked into the school. "Did they break your ribs or anything?"

"Something sure hurts," said Eldon. He winced and grabbed his side. "Those fans sure have a funny way of saying, 'I love you.'"

Annie put her hand on Eldon's shoulder. "I'm sorry. If I'd known this would happen . . ."

Eldon raised his lip and sneered. "It's just part of being famous, sweet pea."

Not much got done at Lincoln that morning. By ten o'clock the crowd outside had tripled, the police had shown up to direct traffic, and a TV crew was setting up their cameras. Most people stood on the sidewalks shading their eyes and staring at the school. Some of them got up onto car roofs and looked through binoculars. A dozen or so climbed into nearby trees. The students stood at the windows and watched the people watching them.

Just before lunch Mrs. Popper called Eldon into her office.

"I've got a problem," said the principal, leaning across her desk. "Know what it is?"

"Me?" said Eldon.

"In a way," said Mrs. Popper. "As long as you're inside this building, there's going to be a crowd outside."

Eldon took out his retainer and set it on the edge of

the desk. Mrs. Popper made a face but didn't say anything. "Why don't you tell the police to make them move?" Eldon suggested.

"For one, they're not doing anything wrong. For two, they're on a public sidewalk. And for three, it wouldn't do any good. They'd only move down the street and wait for you there."

"I imagine that's the truth, ma'm," said Eldon, picking up the retainer. "Some of those people have come a far piece."

Mrs. Popper raised an eyebrow. "They believe you're Elvis, but you and I know differently, right?"

Eldon replaced the retainer and shrugged. "I don't know what to think," he said truthfully.

"I think I may have a plan," said Mrs. Popper. She leaned back in her chair and patted the pile of neatly coiled hair atop her head. "Why don't we give your fans a free concert this afternoon?"

"Why?" asked Eldon. "Won't that make things worse?"

"Because as soon as they hear Eldon Grant sing, they'll know you're not Elvis and they'll go home." Mrs. Popper folded her hands and leaned forward. "What do you think?"

"I don't know what my manager would say about a

free concert," said Eldon. "I've got a career to think about, you know."

"Career? Manager?" said Mrs. Popeye. "You've got a manager?"

"Annie Frootzmacher," said Eldon. "She's my Colonel Tom Parker." He raised his lip and gave her an Elvis sneer. "You know who he is, don't you?"

"No, but I'm sure he's a fine fellow," said Mrs. Popper. She got to her feet and began pacing back and forth behind her desk. "Now listen. We've got to get rid of those people outside, so just go out there and sing them a song. I want them to see the real you."

Eldon narrowed his eyes. "What do you mean the real me?"

Mrs. Popper paused. "You know the one who's . . . ummm, a . . ."

Eldon sighed. Mrs. Popper didn't have to finish the sentence. He knew what she meant. "Okay," he agreed.

After lunch Eldon rolled up the sleeves of his T-shirt and found a string to hold up his sweatpants. Mrs. Rhodes, the AV lady, ran some wires out onto the front steps of the school and set up an amp and a microphone.

At two o'clock the student body filed outside into the sunny spring day and sat down on the lawn. They chattered excitedly among themselves and watched the crew from Channel Six's Action News set up their cameras.

Five minutes later the principal stepped to the microphone and blew her whistle, nearly blasting away her eyeballs.

"Quiet!" she shouted.

"Elvis Presley does not go to this school," announced the principal, her voice booming out over the loudspeaker. "Eldon Grant does, but he's certainly no king of rock and roll."

Henry Botkins shouted, "He's the king of nothing."

"That's right," said Mrs. Popper. "He's the king of nothing. Just your average student with your average talent." She turned and pointed at the big school doors. "And here he is to prove it!"

For a moment everything was silent. People held their breath.

Mrs. Popper stepped to the side. She stared back at the doors. Nothing.

Then suddenly the doors flew open and Eldon exploded onto the steps, waving his guitar.

"It's Elll-visss!" screamed Tammy Wilson.

"It's the King!" yelled Annabelle.

The students rose to their feet. The people who'd been staking out the school surged onto the lawn.

Eldon plugged in his guitar, then stepped up to the microphone and raised his fist.

"Elll-visss!" screamed a hundred voices.

Eldon smiled.

"Elvis! Elvis! Elvis!" they chanted.

Eldon blew the crowd a kiss, and they sent it back with a roar. As he tuned his guitar his toes began to tingle, then his feet, his legs, his body, finally his head. He felt as alive and powerful as he had at the talent show.

Eldon looked into the crowd and smiled. "Glad to be back, folks. Have you missed me?"

The answer rattled the windows.

Mrs. Popper looked about, wringing her hands.

"Hello, Lincoln!" shouted Eldon, thrusting his fist back into the air. "Are you ready to rock?"

"Yes!" everyone screamed back.

"Are you ready to roll?"

"Yes!"

"I can't hear you!"

"Yes!"

"Louder!"

"Yes!"

"LOUDER!"

"YES!"

Blam! "Well now it's one for the money! Two for the show . . ."

The crowd exploded. Mrs. Popper groaned.

Eldon was no average student, and no average talent. He tore through "Blue Suede Shoes" as if he'd been singing it all his life.

Wham! Bam! Zam! The guitar was singing too. Traffic came to a halt. People ran into the street and started to dance.

Eldon shook and strutted up and down the steps.

"Ellll-viss!"

Hundreds of hands reached out to him. Hundreds of voices cried his name. The crew from Action News scrambled to get closer.

"Ellll-viss!"

He tore open his T-shirt.

Tammy Wilson screamed. Annabelle fell to her knees, crying. "It's him! It's him!"

Time stood still. Nothing mattered but the music. People were jumping up and down, turning in circles, crying, yelling, fainting, and singing along to the music.

His guitar and voice were one, finally rising to a frantic finale.

Before the last note had died away, before the

crowd could catch its breath, Eldon dropped to one knee, pulled down the microphone, and eased into his next song, singing, "Love me tender, love me true. Say you'll never go. . . ."

As the words of the ballad drifted over the crowd the dancing stopped, and so did the screaming. Three more people fainted. Annie put a hand to her mouth and choked back a tear.

Mrs. Popper shut her eyes and began to hum softly, remembering the first time she'd heard Elvis sing this song in concert. Annabelle and Irene were holding each other and sobbing softly on the sidewalk. Tammy Wilson had her hands to her cheeks. Even Henry Botkins had been touched. Wide-eyed, he stood frozen, his mouth flopped open like a mailbox door.

Across the lawn and out on the sidewalk people were hypnotized, swaying to the music like palm trees shifting in the breeze. Eldon's voice, low and sweet, wrapped itself around them.

As the end approached, Eldon dropped a hand from the guitar, closed his eyes, and reached out to the crowd. "So my darling I love you . . . and I always will."

The last note faded and for a moment there was silence. Eldon lifted his head. He was crying.

The applause began, slowly at first, then building till the sound pounded against Eldon's chest. He took a deep breath, got to his feet, grinned, then raised his guitar in triumph.

"Thank you, Lincoln. You've been very kind."

He put a hand to his lips and blew the crowd a kiss.

"Ellll-vis!" they screamed.

More people fainted.

Eldon waved his guitar and bent over the microphone. "See you all around now," he said. "God bless you, folks, God bless you."

Everyone was jumping up and down and waving their arms. They didn't want him to go.

"One more song! One more song!" they chanted.

But Eldon was tired, more tired than he could ever remember being in his life. He unplugged the guitar, then walked back up the stairs and stood at the top for a moment, waving.

"Thank you, thank you much," he said. Then he pushed through the doors, and was gone.

10

WORLD FAMOUS

 Eldon spent the next four days at home. Not only did he need the rest, but the school administrators decided it would be best if Eldon kept off the school grounds for a while.

"It sounds crazy," he told his mother one morning over his third bowl of grits. "But I'm so tired all the time. I feel like I'm forty instead of twelve."

"You've gone through a lot," said Eldon's mom. "Anybody would be exhausted."

"Perhaps, but I ain't just anybody," said Eldon.

Apparently, a lot of people agreed.

During the week Eldon's home was flooded with cards and letters and gifts as word of his story and pictures of his performance were beamed around the world. Every day the mail carrier brought a sack of mail. Lots of people sent teddy bears too. Obviously, Eldon's mom wasn't the only one who liked the song "Teddy Bear."

"Won't you be my teddy bear?" said the note attached to one. It was signed, "Your old pal, Annabelle."

A steady stream of visitors stopped by as well.

Mrs. Popper came over, bug eyes and all. Tammy Wilson sneaked in with a box of homemade chocolate chip cookies. Annie came on Wednesday with a clipping from the paper.

"Guess what! They've made you the star of the Elvis impersonator contest at the Mayfair Mall!"

Eldon shook his head. "I'm not quite sure who I am, Annie. But I do know I'm not an Elvis impersonator.

"I know that, and so do the people at the mall," Annie told him. "They want you there as Elvis! You're going to judge the contest. They're going to give you five thousand dollars just for showing up."

"Five thousand dollars!" said Eldon. "You're kidding."

"Nope," said Annie. "Five thousand big ones."

Eldon stared at her. "What kind of manager are you? I ought to be getting twice that. And when are you going to book me on the *Ed Sullivan Show*?"

It was Annie's turn to stare at Eldon. "The *Ed Sullivan Show* has been off the air for years," said Annie. "Ed Sullivan's dead."

"Dead?" Eldon shut his eyes, trying to clear his head. Who was Ed Sullivan anyway? Why had he just said that to Annie?

Annie pulled out her little book. "Elvis got famous appearing on Ed Sullivan's TV show," she said. "I'm trying to book you on MTV."

Eldon's eyes flew open. "Then get me on there. Quick," he said. "Time's a wasting, sweet pea. The world needs to know I'm back."

Annie glanced around at the piles of mail and stacks of teddy bears. "That's one thing I wouldn't worry about, Eldon. It looks to me as if the word is out."

11

HENRY BOTKINS

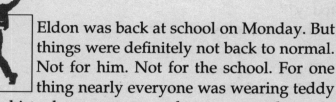 Eldon was back at school on Monday. But things were definitely not back to normal. Not for him. Not for the school. For one thing nearly everyone was wearing teddy bear T-shirts, baggy pants, and orange sneakers. At least twenty kids had been fitted for retainers.

The moment he stepped through the school doors he was attacked.

"Elvis!" the students squealed, swarming around him, like bees to honey.

Everyone wanted his autograph. Even Henry Botkins.

"I'm your biggest fan," he said, pushing his notebook through the crowd. "Just sign it to your best friend, me."

"Be my pleasure," said Eldon. He gave Henry a baffled look. "What's your name, son?"

"He . . . He . . . Henry," he stammered, his face turning red. "Don't you remember?"

Eldon shook his head. "I don't believe we've ever met," he said. Then he wrote, "To Henry, Yours truly Elvis Presley." He winked and returned the notebook. "You take care now, young fella."

Everyone giggled. Henry hurried away.

Eldon smiled at all the girls. "How are you ladies today?"

The ladies giggled.

Eldon wiggled his hips.

The girls squealed.

Eldon raised his lip in an Elvis sneer, then started to sing a Presley song. "Hey don't be cruel, oooh, oh, oh. To a heart that's true . . ."

"That's my favorite song!" screamed Angela Barnes, throwing her arms around him. "I love it! I love you!"

"Angela, get hold of yourself!" shouted Annie. She grabbed her from behind and pulled her off Eldon. "You're in school."

"Annie, it's really all right," said Eldon, his eyes fixed on Angela. Had she really said she loved him?

"Come along," said Annie, taking him by the arm. "You'll be late for class."

"Elvis, please! Don't go!" begged some of the girls.

Annie gave them a look of disgust. "Leeches," she muttered.

"Elvis, if you leave I'll check right into the Heartbreak Hotel," said Angela.

"Please do. Just don't ever check out," said Annie. She tugged Eldon's arm. "Come along. We're late for class."

"Elll-viss!" everyone wailed as Annie hauled him away.

"Parasites," she said, glancing back over her shoulder. "I never should have allowed you to come to school today."

In history Mrs. Hanson couldn't seem to keep her eyes off Eldon or her mind off Elvis.

"Since we have such an honored guest with us today, maybe we should talk about the history of rock and roll instead of the Civil War."

The class applauded.

Mrs. Hanson was wearing a tight, polka-dotted suit and a little blue bow tie that matched the color of her big round eyes. "Tell us, Elvis, was it fun making all those movies?"

"I don't rightly know," said Eldon.

"I guess that means sometimes it was fun, sometimes it wasn't," said Mrs. Hanson. She looked around the room. "Class. I hope you're taking notes."

Mrs. Hanson continued. "What's your favorite song?"

"I'm not sure," said Eldon.

"That's a song I haven't heard," said Mrs. Hanson. "But, believe me, I plan to get a copy."

"This is a waste of our time," whispered Annie, leaning across the aisle. "Let's go down to the mall. We need to sign the contract for the Elvis judging."

"We can't cut school," said Eldon.

"So, Mr. Presley, is there anything you've learned that you'd like to share with the class?"

"Come on, Eldon," Annie whispered.

"Momma always said education is the most important thing someone can have, and I believe her," Eldon said.

"Such a wise answer!" said Mrs. Hanson. She put a hand alongside her cheek, closed her eyes, and sighed dreamily. "And to think some people used to put down Elvis for setting a bad example. Little did they know how much he valued school."

After a few more minutes of answering Mrs. Hanson's questions, Eldon grew bored. He glanced over at Annie. She'd obviously given up on Eldon. Her biography of Elvis was propped open inside her history notebook and she was reading while Mrs. Hanson droned on.

Why do I need school? Eldon thought suddenly. I'm already a big star. "Annie," he whispered. "Let's get out of here!"

She grinned, then flashed him a thumbs-up sign. As soon as history class was over, the two of them caught the number ten bus to the mall.

12

TRUANTS

The Mayfair Mall was at the other end of Lincoln, and the bus made a lot of stops. Along the way Annie pasted a new tattoo onto her cheek, a blue and gold drawing of Elvis holding a microphone.

"What do you think?" she said, studying the tattoo in a little hand mirror.

"I think he's a good-looking fella," said Eldon. "Angela thinks so too."

Annie clucked her tongue. "You may sound like Elvis, and you may feel like him too. But you still look like Eldon Grant."

"What's that supposed to mean?" said Eldon.

"Nothing," said Annie.

"I think it means you're jealous," said Eldon.

"What are you—crazy?" Annie snapped.

Eldon grinned, then looked out the bus window.

By the time they reached the giant pink and white Mayfair Mall it was ten o'clock. The stores were just starting to open. Aside from a few people in jogging outfits, three women with baby strollers, and a lumpy guard sitting on a bench eating a donut, the place was deserted. The smell of coffee and floor wax mingled in the air with the sound of violins flowing from the mall's ceiling speakers.

"Hey, look at this," said Annie, pointing at the Fashion Parade clothing store. "They're getting ready for you."

Across the top of the window someone had taped up a big banner that said:

THE KING IS BACK!
THIS SATURDAY THE NEW ELVIS WILL BE
JUDGING HIS IMPERSONATORS! DON'T MISS
THIS LAST CHANCE TO SEE THOSE WHO KEPT
HIS LEGEND ALIVE WHILE HE WAS GONE!

Under the sign two mannequins were dressed identically in teddy bear T-shirts, baggy pants, and orange sneakers.

"Cool clothes," said Eldon.

"Soon the whole world will be dressing like you," said Annie. "Early next week I'm going to set up an international tour. I wouldn't be surprised if we made a billion dollars."

Eldon nodded. "First thing I'm going to do is buy myself a big two-story house with white columns in the front, a huge front yard, fancy iron gates, and a complete gym and karate studio inside." Eldon chopped the air with his hands. "I'm a karate expert, you know."

"I've read that you are," said Annie. "You know, in Memphis, Tennessee, there's a house just like the one you described. It's called Graceland."

"By golly, I'll buy it!" said Eldon. "Find out who owns it."

Before Annie could answer, someone clamped a hand onto her shoulder, onto Eldon's, too.

"What are you doing out of school!"

Eldon and Annie turned their heads. It was the mall security guard, the lumpy-faced man they'd seen eating a donut. "Where are your parents?"

"We're here on business," said Annie. She glanced over her shoulder at the guard's hand. "Do you mind?"

The guard grunted and removed his hand, dropping it onto a tiny gun strapped to his waist.

"I'm warning you, though. Try to run and I'll shoot."

Annie rolled her eyes. "Now, Sergeant Fish," she said, reading the guard's name off his plastic badge. "Would you really shoot someone for skipping school?"

"You bet," he said. "You're a danger to me, a danger to the mall, and a danger to yourself." He leaned forward, straining the buttons on his too-tight uniform. "It's a fact, most murderers started off as truants."

"Come on, mister. You can't put a hole in someone just because they're not in school," drawled Eldon.

Sergeant Fish patted his gun. "This wouldn't put a hole in anybody. It doesn't shoot bullets. It's a taser. It shoots a dart attached to a wire. It stuns you with electricity." He snorted. "The mall doesn't let me carry bullets."

Thank goodness, thought Eldon.

"As I said, we've got business," said Annie. "We're looking for the manager. Now if you'll tell us where she is."

"I'll do better than that," said Sergeant Fish. "I'll

take you there. I'm sure Miss Abel will want to talk to both your parents and the police."

"You know I could have your job for this," said Annie.

"I've heard that before," said Sergeant Fish. He pointed down the hallway. "Let's go. And don't try anything funny, either."

"We couldn't try anything that would be funnier than you," muttered Eldon.

"What did you say?" asked Fish sharply.

"Nothing," said Eldon, glancing nervously at the taser gun.

The sergeant led Annie and Eldon down to the end of the mall and through a red door marked EMPLOYEES ONLY.

Inside there was a large office crowded with desks overflowing with coffee cups and paper. Behind every desk sat someone with a phone to their ear. The mall manager, Kathy Abel, was at the back of the room, her face buried in the third drawer of a filing cabinet.

"Miss Abel!" shouted the guard over the noise of her chattering employees. "Look what I caught!"

Miss Abel's head came out of the drawer. She squinted across the room through thick glasses.

"What is it this time, Fish?" she asked wearily.

"Truants," said the sergeant. He waved at Eldon and Annie. "I caught them sneaking around in front of the Fashion Parade."

"We weren't sneaking around," said Annie.

"I figure they were waiting to murder the clerk," said Sergeant Fish. "Should we call the police?"

Annie rolled her eyes, grabbed Eldon's hand, and marched across the room to Miss Abel.

"We've talked on the phone," she said, extending her hand. "I'm Annie Frootzmacher, Mr. Presley's manager."

Eldon nodded. "And I'm Presley, ma'm."

Miss Abel's dark eyes widened. She grinned. "Why isn't this a pleasure now?" she said, taking Annie's hand.

She turned to Eldon and smiled sweetly.

"You know I grew up in Memphis," she said with a Southern accent just as strong as Eldon's. "I can't tell you how many times I've been out to Graceland."

"Graceland!" said Eldon. "That's the place I'm going to buy."

Miss Abel laughed and patted Eldon's cheek. "Graceland, of course, was Elvis's home. Oh my, but don't you have the best sense of humor!"

"Elvis's old house is the one I want to buy," said Eldon.

"And that voice. I'd recognize it anywhere."

"He's one hundred percent him, just like the papers and TV reported," said Annie. She slapped Eldon on the back. "You wanted Elvis Presley, well, here he is." She smiled. "Where do we sign the contract?"

"Whoa there! Hold up a minute there!" said Sergeant Fish, hurrying through the desks. "Did I hear you say Elvis Presley?"

"That's right," said Miss Abel.

Sergeant Fish whipped an envelope out of his pocket. "I've been looking for that guy. Where can I find him?"

Eldon laughed. "I guess I know where he is."

"Perfect, then you can deliver this message," said the sergeant, handing over the envelope. "I found it stuck to the window of the Fashion Parade this morning."

Across the front in big letters someone had scrawled, "Deliver to Elvis Presley—Extremely Urgent!"

"This is exciting," said Eldon. He opened it up and took out a three-by-five card.

"So what is it?" asked Annie. "A fan letter?"

"No, ma'm," said Eldon as he scanned the card. His face grew pale. "It's a death threat!"

13

THE DEVIL'S WORK

YOU ARE HURTING OUR CHILDREN.
YOU SHOULD HAVE STAYED DEAD.
THAT'S WHERE YOU BELONG!

Eldon read the words in a shaky voice, then handed the card to Sergeant Fish.

"I'll find out who sent this," said the sergeant. He held the note against his face and squinted.

"What are you doing?" asked Miss Abel.

"Checking for fingerprints," he said.

Annie rolled her eyes.

"Why would someone write this?" said Eldon. "Elvis hasn't hurt anyone."

"Some folks believe rock and roll is the tool of the devil," said Miss Abel. "They think Elvis and his music will ruin their children's lives."

"The devil? But Elvis loves children," said Eldon.

"Don't worry, most people do love the King. You'll find that out on Saturday when thousands of them show up to see you onstage in our parking lot," said Miss Abel. "Believe me. This place is going to go crazy."

"And that means Elvis is going to need plenty of police protection," said Annie. "As his manager, I insist you provide a bodyguard."

"I'll keep an eye on him," said Sergeant Fish, quickly raising his hand. "I've always wanted to be a bodyguard."

"I don't know," Annie said slowly.

"Sergeant Fish is our most trusted employee," said Miss Abel. "You'll have nothing to worry about with him on the job."

Eldon and Annie exchanged worried looks.

"Maybe we don't really need a bodyguard," said Annie.

"I insist," said Miss Abel. "Elvis's appearance is the biggest thing we've ever done."

"But. . . ." said Eldon, shooting another glance at Sergeant Fish.

"No arguing," said Miss Abel. "We can't risk Elvis's death. It would ruin everything."

"I agree with you on that," said Eldon.

"Then it's settled." Sergeant Fish saluted. "I'm on the job!" He looked around. "Okay, where can I find him?"

"Find who?" asked Miss Abel.

"Elvis Presley," said Sergeant Fish. "Isn't that who I'm supposed to guard?"

"He's right here," said Miss Abel, pointing at Eldon. "Haven't you been paying attention?"

Sergeant Fish gave Eldon a curious look. "You're Elvis?"

Eldon sighed.

"Guard him with your life," said Miss Abel.

Sergeant Fish saluted again. "Don't worry! I'm on the job!"

14

A LONG NIGHT

That night Mrs. Grant set an extra place at the table.

"These sure are tasty mashed potatoes," said Sergeant Fish, waving a spoonful at Mrs. Grant. "Will there be seconds?"

"I'm sorry," said Mrs. Grant. "If I'd have known you were coming, I . . ."

"That's all right," mumbled the sergeant through a mouthful of potatoes. "I'll double up on dessert."

"We don't usually eat dessert," said Mrs. Grant.

The sergeant's mouth flopped open, displaying the mashed potatoes. Eldon turned quickly away.

"I'm sorry," said Mrs. Grant.

"It's okay," said the sergeant. "Bodyguard work is often dangerous, and never easy."

"Well, I want you to know how much Eldon and I appreciate what you're doing," said Mrs. Grant. She shuddered. "Oooo. When I think of that death threat."

"Annie said we'd better get used to them," said Eldon. "According to her book Elvis got at least two a week."

Mrs. Grant choked back her tears. "Oh, Eldon, I wish all this had never happened."

"What are you talking about, Momma?" Eldon reached out and patted his mother's hand. "I'm doing this all for you. After I get you a Cadillac and a mink coat, I'm buying you a new house right next door to me in Memphis."

Mrs. Grant's head came out of her hands. "Memphis?"

"You're going to love Tennessee," said Eldon.

"Tennessee? But this is our home! All our friends and relatives live here," said Mrs. Grant.

"I'll move them too," said Eldon. "Momma, I'm going to be a billionaire."

"I wish your father was here," said Mrs. Grant. "He'd know what to say." She sighed.

"Please, don't worry. I know what I'm doing. I'm the King, Momma. Nothing can harm me."

"That's probably just what Elvis thought," said

Mrs. Grant. "And you know that he died a young man."

Eldon didn't say anything. Between Miss Lilly's warning and that terrible death threat, he couldn't stop worrying about what lay ahead for him.

To make matters worse, Sergeant Fish followed Eldon everywhere. Even when Eldon went into the bathroom, he was right outside.

"Are you okay?" he called every thirty seconds.

"I'm doing fine, Sarge," Eldon grumbled.

That night Sergeant Fish slept at the foot of Eldon's bed, curled up in a sleeping bag. His taser gun was strapped to his side.

"Good night," whispered the sergeant. "If you need anything, just call."

"I need a good night's sleep," said Eldon. "I'm so tired."

"I'll make sure you're not disturbed," said the sergeant.

"Thanks," said Eldon.

"Sweet dreams," said Sergeant Fish.

Eldon put his hands behind his head, sank back into his pillow, and closed his eyes. Soon he had drifted off into dreams of rock and roll concerts, limousines, and world travels.

"*Ga-rah! Gaa-rah!*"

"Ba-rap! Ba-rap!"

"Ba-rap! Ga-rah! Ba-rap!"

A steady noise awoke Eldon. *"Ba-rap! Ga-rah! Ba-rap! Ga-rah!"*

It sounded like the slime creatures from the swamp-sucker movies. Something was in his room, something awful.

He sat straight up in bed. "S . . . s . . . sarge," he whispered.

"Ba-rap! Glurp! Glurp! Ba-rop!"

Eldon gulped. Maybe the thing had already eaten Sergeant Fish!

Barely breathing, he crawled to the edge of the bed and peered over.

"Ba-rah! Barah! Ger-lurp!"

"Sergeant Fish!" Eldon sighed and rolled his eyes. "Wake up! You're snoring like a monster!"

Sergeant Fish's eyes snapped open. "Monster!" he yelled, reaching for his taser. "Hit the floor!"

Eldon sighed again. "The monster is you."

"Huh?" said Sergeant Fish.

Eldon grumbled. "Your snoring woke me up."

"Isn't that funny. I wake up my wife all the time too!"

"It's not funny," said Eldon. "I told you how tired I was. In fact I—"

Sca-reech! Outside a car skidded to halt.

A second later there was a shout, and a second after that a window downstairs shattered with a roar.

Kerash!

Eldon gasped. From somewhere down the hallway Mrs. Grant screamed.

Sergeant Fish and Eldon ran to the window.

Sca-reech! They got there just as a white Lincoln, its lights off, sped away.

"Don't leave this room!" said Sergeant Fish. He drew his taser and ran for the door. "I'll be right back."

Eldon stood in the doorway of the darkened room, his head and heart pounding, while Sergeant Fish stumbled about the living room.

"Ouch! Ow! Ouchie!" a voice called from downstairs.

"Who's there?" his mother demanded.

"Just me," replied Sergeant Fish. "Be careful, ma'm. There's lots of glass. Whoops! Whoa! Ouch!"

To Eldon it seemed like the sergeant was gone forever. When he finally returned he was with Mrs. Grant. He switched on the lights and handed Eldon a brick.

"This is what came through the window."

"Who would want to do such a thing?" asked Mrs.

Grant. She wrapped her arms around her pink robe and shivered. "What are they after?"

"Me," said Eldon. He held up the brick and showed his mom the words scrawled over the rough red surface:

GO AWAY, ELVIS! OR ELSE!

15

WORLD TOUR

Eldon didn't leave the house once for the next four days. He couldn't. A crowd of fans and reporters had the place surrounded. There must have been at least a thousand of them milling around, with more arriving every hour. The street had been blocked off and all the TV networks had parked huge trucks along the curb with television cameras mounted on their roofs. At least a dozen people were manning carts selling everything from hot dogs and pretzels to T-shirts saying: I SAW ELVIS'S HOUSE!

Helicopters circled overhead constantly and the phone never stopped ringing. Seated at the kitchen table Eldon must have given at least a hundred phone interviews. Some of the callers tried to trip him up with questions about his past.

"What kind of a car did Elvis give his girl friend in 1974?" asked someone. "Answer that!"

"A 1971 De Tomaso Pantera," Eldon snapped back. "Next question!"

"What did he give his friend and drummer D. J. Fontana?"

"A diamond horseshoe ring!" said Eldon. "How about something harder?"

He couldn't believe he knew all the answers. A couple of weeks ago Eldon hadn't even known what Graceland was. Now he seemed to know every detail of Elvis Presley's life. Eldon had given up on trying to figure out what had happened to him on the day of the talent show. All he knew was something inside him had changed so that he walked and talked, and, best of all, sang like a rock and roll legend.

"When Elvis was little, what did he promise his momma?" asked another caller.

"Easy. He said he'd buy her a Cadillac," said Eldon. "And I did." He winked across the table at his mother. "And I will again."

Every call was for Eldon. Most were from fans, many were from reporters, and one was from the person who had smashed his window.

"I'm warning you!" he screamed. "Next time it won't just be a brick. Don't you realize? You're killing my kids! Show up at that Elvis contest on Saturday and you're a goner. That's a promise!"

Before Eldon could stammer out a reply, the man hung up.

Eldon winced.

"Maybe you shouldn't judge that contest on Saturday," mumbled Sergeant Fish. His mouth was full of a tuna and bologna sandwich he'd just made. "I'm not sure I can protect you."

"Don't worry. He's not going to that mall," said Mrs. Grant. She reached across the table and took her son's hand. "He'll be staying right here with me till it's safe to go outside."

"That could be years, ma'm," said Sergeant Fish.

"I don't care," said Mrs. Grant. "It's too dangerous out there for my baby. I don't care if we're locked up in this house for the rest of our lives. I've already lost one member of my family—I'm not going to lose another."

Eldon looked at his mom, then over at Sergeant Fish. A hunk of tuna was hanging off his chin, like some gooey gray Christmas ornament.

"Momma, I can't," said Eldon. "I've signed a contract. Elvis always keeps his word."

"But you're not Elvis," said Mrs. Grant.

Eldon raised his lip and sneered. "Of course I'm Elvis."

Blam! Suddenly the kitchen door burst open.

Eldon spun around in his chair. Mrs. Grant screamed. Sergeant Fish dropped his sandwich and whipped out his taser gun. "Freeze!" he cried, aiming it at the intruder as she came charging through the door.

"Whoa! It's only me," said Annie, skidding to a stop. She held up a gold lamé suit. "Put that gun away. I'm just delivering Eldon's costume for tomorrow's show."

Sergeant Fish eyed her for a moment, then grunted and lowered his gun. "Next time, knock," he mumbled.

Annie smiled politely as she hurried over to Eldon. She held up the costume and waved it before his eyes. "Great news! They want you in Japan next month. Three shows, three cities." She grinned and tossed the costume onto his lap. "One million bucks!"

"Yes!" said Eldon. He gave the air a karate chop, then raised his thumb. "A million dollars!"

"I already signed the contract." She looked from face to face. "Isn't this great?"

"You bet it is," said Eldon. "I'll be back on top in no

96

time." He gave his mother a giant grin and winked. "This calls for a celebration. Momma, break out the good glasses and a bottle of champagne."

Mrs. Grant gasped. "Champagne?"

"Eldon, you don't drink," said Annie.

Eldon paused. He looked around, confused.

"Drinking was one of Elvis's problems," said Annie.

"Oh, yeah, now I remember," said Eldon, wrinkling his face.

Mrs. Grant looked at her son with horror. "I'm calling Miss Lilly," she said. "I want my boy back. Maybe she knows what to do."

Eldon narrowed his eyes. "I wouldn't do that, Momma."

"Don't tell me what to do," said Mrs. Grant, crossing to the phone. "I'm your mother."

Eldon came over and put his hand on top of his mother's. "I'm warning you, Momma. If you call Miss Lilly, you're going to be very, very sorry."

"Eldon!" Mrs. Grant said. "What's gotten into you? Where is the Eldon I know and love?"

"He's on his way to ruling the world of rock and roll," said Eldon. He chuckled. "And this time nothing is going to stop me. Not you, not that nut Miss Lilly. Not anyone."

"Don't tell that to the crazies who are trying to kill you," said Sergeant Fish.

"No one's going to kill me," said Eldon. "No one would dare strike down the King."

Sergeant Fish nervously fingered his taser gun. "But Eldon . . ."

"This mall job is going to get me a lot of publicity," said Eldon. "I need it. Nothing better go wrong tomorrow at the show. Got it?"

"You're the boss," said the sergeant.

"I'm the boss, *sir*," he said. "Got that too?"

Sergeant Fish swallowed. "Yes, sir."

Mrs. Grant was crying. "Whatever happened to the sweet boy with the baggy pants and the retainer? The one who always had a smile for his friends and a hug for his mom?" She sniffled and wiped her eyes. "Where did he go?"

Eldon smiled. "Don't worry, ma'm. Wherever he is I'm sure he's doing just fine."

16

NUT CASES

 On Saturday Eldon squeezed into the gold suit, wrapped his Artist of the Year belt around his waist, and put on a pair of sunglasses.

"Ready to rock, ready to roll, and ready to reclaim my crown," he told himself, striking a pose in front of the mirror.

At eleven o'clock a limousine arrived. Annie was already inside. The police cleared a path and Eldon, his mother, and Sergeant Fish sprinted out of the house and into the waiting car.

As it pulled away, the crowd screamed and aimed their cameras. There was a burst of flashbulbs when Eldon stuck his head out the window and waved.

"Ya'll come see my show now!"

As the car sped through the streets of town, Eldon worked on his hair, stacking it up, then pulling a few strands forward over his eye.

"I'm one good-looking guy, if I say so myself," he said. "Girls, look out!"

"Maybe I ought to warn Angela Barnes," said Annie. "I'm not sure egomaniacs are her type."

"Angela Barnes?" Eldon laughed. "You think I'd want to waste my time with that little girl? My next date is going to be with a movie star."

Annie shook her head.

"I wish you didn't have to appear before all those people," Mrs. Grant said again. "It's too dangerous."

"Just stick close to Sergeant Fish," Annie advised. "We're not going to get that million bucks for the Japan tour if you're dead."

"Please don't talk like that." Mrs. Grant wrung her hands. "Oh, we should have stayed at home. I just know it, I do."

"Momma, if you don't stop that whining I'm going to throw you out of the car," said Eldon. "Do you hear me?"

"But Eldon—" said Mrs. Grant.

"Shut up!" said Eldon. His eyes narrowed. "I've got a zillion things to worry about right now and I need a little quiet. All right?"

Mrs. Grant chewed on her knuckles and nodded. "All right, son. All right."

"And don't call me son, either," he muttered, turning away.

Mrs. Grant sniffled. Sergeant Fish patted her hand. "This is a tough day for all of us," he whispered.

"He's just nervous," whispered Annie.

"The boy needs a father. He left us so suddenly, there wasn't even time for a good-bye," said Mrs. Grant. She sighed and stared off, tears filling her eyes. "And to think we fell in love to Elvis's songs. My husband and I thought he was the greatest. How could he have done this to me?"

"Things will be better after the concert," whispered Annie, leaning over. "Elvis was often in a bad mood before one of his shows."

Eldon turned and gave them a sharp look. No one talked the rest of the way to the mall.

The Mayfair Mall was just off Highway 16. As they pulled into the giant parking lot, the limousine driver lowered the window between the front seat and the back. "Miss Abel wants me to bring you around through the rear," he said. "The mall's closed for the show so only you and the impersonators will be inside. It's all for your security, of course."

"I wouldn't expect anything less," said Eldon.

"You can't be too careful," said the driver. He was wearing a little black cap and gold-rimmed sunglasses. "The world is full of nut cases."

"Ain't that the truth, though," said Eldon.

"Ain't it, though," echoed Annie.

"Any idea how many folks they're expecting today?" asked Eldon.

"Tons," said the driver. "About a thousand people camped out last night just to get good seats. Miss Abel said we might have twenty thousand people here today, maybe more."

Annie whistled.

"We ought to have a hundred thousand," said Eldon. "Don't they know I'm going to be onstage?" He snorted with disgust.

Annie and Mrs. Grant looked at one another but didn't say anything. No matter what they told him, Eldon obviously wasn't going to be convinced that there was a big enough crowd.

A few moments later the driver brought the car to a halt alongside the curb at the rear of the mall.

"Looks like you've got a welcoming committee," said the driver over his shoulder.

"Miss Abel?" asked Annie.

"A mob of fans?" asked Mrs. Grant.

"Assassins?" asked Sergeant Fish.

Eldon rolled down the window and four faces peered inside.

"Whoa!" said Annie. "It's Elvis Presley. Times four!"

17

TOO MANY PRESLEYS

"You all better get inside before those Elvis freaks out front discover you're here," said an Elvis in a leather jacket.

An Elvis in a blue jumpsuit opened the limousine door. "Let's go, folks."

Eldon, Annie, Mrs. Grant, and Sergeant Fish piled out of the limousine. They followed the four Elvis Presleys into the mall through a door marked Service Entrance.

Miss Abel was waiting inside.

She leaned over and gave Eldon a kiss on the cheek. "I'm so glad to see you!" She giggled.

"My pleasure, ma'm," said Eldon, wiping his cheek.

Miss Abel composed herself and gestured to the four Presley imitators standing to her side.

"This is Don, John, Carl, and Burt," she said. "They're the imitators you'll be judging today."

Don, the Elvis in the leather jacket, sneered. "Doesn't it seem kind of strange that the Elvis who doesn't look like Elvis is judging the ones who do?"

"Yeah, real strange," said the other three. Every one of them wore huge sideburns. Don and Carl looked like they had on wigs.

Eldon raised his lip and sneered at them. "Looks like I'm about to put you good ol' boys out of business, don't it?"

"We'll see about that," said Carl. He was wearing wraparound sunglasses and a ton of gold chains. "We aren't ready to retire just yet. If you're really Elvis, you're going to have to prove it."

Eldon eyed Carl with contempt.

"Just because you get in the papers doesn't make you the genuine article," said John. On his hand there was a tattoo of a singing Elvis. It looked just like the one on Annie's cheek, except it was real. "Like Carl says, you got to prove it."

"And I will, this afternoon," said Eldon. "I'm going to sing a few little songs after you boys finish your lame imitations. That is, if you don't object, Miss Abel."

"Object!" said Miss Abel. "The mall would be

honored. Why, you'll be on television all over the world."

Eldon touched his forehead. "That's the whole idea, ma'm."

The Elvis quartet exchanged worried looks and grumbled among themselves.

"The show starts in ten minutes," said Miss Abel. "Carl, Don, John, and Burt go on in that order. Elvis, you'll come on last and do the judging."

"My pleasure," said Eldon, nodding.

"Nervous?" asked Mrs. Grant, placing her hand on Eldon's shoulder.

Eldon looked over at his mother's hand. "Do you mind? This suit is brand new."

Mrs. Grant quickly removed her hand.

"If you need anything, just holler," said Annie. "That's the manager's job."

Eldon ignored Annie and turned to Miss Abel. "Where might I find my dressing room?"

"Ummm . . . umm," stammered Miss Abel. "Dressing room?"

"You have heard of dressing rooms, haven't you?" said Eldon.

Miss Abel swallowed. "I'm sorry. We just didn't have time. Umm . . . would one of the bathrooms be okay?"

"Not hardly." Eldon looked around, tapped his foot, and sighed loudly.

"We're truly sorry," said Miss Abel.

Eldon grumbled, then stormed off down the center of the mall, heading for the nearest rest room.

Sergeant Fish trailed behind, keeping his eyes open for Elvis assassins.

Eldon stomped past the Fashion Parade, Mr. Paperback, the Music Factory, and the Merry Nut and Candy Shoppe. An old man, as thin as a toothpick, was mopping the floor just outside the bathroom. He raised his head as Eldon thundered past him and kicked open the door.

"I'll wait outside," shouted Sergeant Fish, waddling along, far behind. "Won't nobody get by me!"

But before the words were out of his mouth, the four Elvises skidded around the old man and his bucket of soapy water and wax, and flung open the door. It nearly snapped off its hinges.

Ka-bang!

"Look out!" yelled the old man.

Eldon was bending over the sink when the Presley boys came charging in.

He raised his wet, soapy face and eyed them with disgust. "If you want an autograph, get in line with everyone else."

No one moved. Carl took off his glasses and polished them on his flowered shirt.

Eldon turned. "Didn't you hear me? Leave. I don't want anything, or anyone, screwing up my new career. Understand?"

"Boy, you really are something, aren't you?" said Carl. "Your career? What about our careers?"

"What about your stupid careers?" said Eldon.

The Elvises pressed in closer, backing him against the sink.

"You know we made a pretty good living till you showed up," said John. He was picking at his teeth with his fingernail, displaying his Elvis tattoo.

"We were doing real good," added Carl. "Then you had to come along."

Eldon gulped.

"No one is going to want to see an imitator when the real thing is just down the street," said Don, poking Eldon in the chest.

"We've got families to feed," said Burt. He leaned over till he was nose to nose with Eldon. "Don't you realize? You're hurting our children!"

Eldon winced. He'd heard that somewhere before.

Bam! John pounded his fist into his palm. "How are my kids going to eat if you put me out of business?"

Eldon looked around the cold, white-tiled room for

a quick way out. *Bam! Bam! Bam!* The other Elvises pounded their fists too.

"We warned you. This time it won't just be a brick!" *Bam! Bam! Bam! Bam!* Four fists pounded four palms.

Eldon raised his hands and forced a smile. "Hey, take it easy now."

Whap! Don slapped Eldon's ear. "We're done taking it easy!"

"Ouch!" Eldon's ear was ringing like a Chinese gong. "Stop it! What do you think you're—"

Whop! A hand clamped over his mouth.

"You're going to have the shortest comeback in history," said Burt, tightening his grip on Eldon's face.

Eldon's heart was pounding. His stomach was doing flips. His eyes looked ready to blast from their sockets.

"Finish him off," said Don coldly.

"Return to sender," said John. "Remember that song, Elvis?" He laughed.

Burt laughed too, loosening his hand just enough for Eldon to bite it. "Ouch!" he bellowed, yanking it away. "Why you little . . ."

"Sergeant Fish!" screamed Eldon. "Help! Help!"

Every Elvis spun toward the door. But when no one came charging through, they spun back toward the sink. Eldon snarled and raised a hand in front of his face.

Blam! He kicked Burt in the shin, then caught Don with an elbow to the ribs.

"Ow!"

"Ooof!"

The Elvises had forgotten Elvis was a karate expert.

Wham! A fist to Burt's stomach. *Bam!* A kick to Carl's knee. *Whap!* A chop to John's ribs.

"Ugh!"

"Ow!"

"Oooo!"

The men reeled back. Eldon sprinted out of the bathroom.

"Hey, Fish!" he screamed, spotting the sergeant drooling over the goodies displayed in the window of the Merry Nut and Candy Shoppe. "Help!"

The sergeant turned just as Eldon plowed into the old man's bucket of soapy water.

Blam!

The bucket went flying. So did Eldon. Face first, he went skidding across the wet floor.

"Whoa! Oh! Heeeelllp!"

Ka-blam! He slammed, shoulder first, into the gate outside the Fashion Parade.

"Ooooof!" The blow momentarily stunned him.

A moment later, one, two, three, four Elvis Presleys came charging out of the bathroom and smack into the same soapy mess.

"Oh!"

"No!"

"Ooops!"

"Yikes!"

Swish! Swoosh! Across the floor they went on their backs and stomachs. Don's wig went flying. Burt lost a blue suede shoe. Carl sucked up a mouthful of suds.

"Ugh!"

"Ooooof!"

"Ow!"

"Yuck!"

One after another they skidded into poor Eldon, slamming him again and again into the Fashion Parade gate.

"Look what you've done to my floor!" screamed the old man, waving his mop like a sword.

The five Presleys struggled to untangle themselves.

"Yo!"

"Off my face!"

"Ouch!"

"Get your foot out of there!"

For a few moments they flopped about in a wad of jumpsuits, gold chains, sideburns, and soapy wax.

"Freeze Presleys!" said Sergeant Fish, pointing his taser at the wriggling mass. "I won't warn you twice!"

Carl squinted. "Ignore him. It's only a toy gun."

"A toy?" said Sergeant Fish indignantly. "No way. This happens to be a powerful electric pistol that—"

"Take it back to the joke shop," said Carl. He laughed and pushed himself up onto his elbow.

"I won't warn you three times!" said Sergeant Fish, waving the gun about wildly. "I'll shoot. I will!"

Carl laughed and rolled onto his knees.

Sergeant Fish's hand was bouncing about like a ship in a storm.

"I won't warn you a fourth time!"

Bam! The gun suddenly went off. No one looked more surprised than Sergeant Fish. A silver dart, trailing a thin copper wire, came shooting from the barrel.

Whap! It plunged into Eldon's neck and stuck.

Zap! A jolt of electricity shot into his body. His hair leapt to attention. His tongue came out in a silent scream. His eyes tried to leave their sockets.

The four Presleys were too stunned to move.

"Wow!" said Burt.

Eldon tried to grab for the dart, but his hands wouldn't obey his commands. His body was flopping about like a fish on a pier.

Carl turned to John. "Whoa! I guess that isn't a toy!"

"I got to get me one of those," said Don.

"Help him!" screamed Annie, hurrying toward the commotion.

"My boy!" cried Mrs. Grant, racing down the mall. "What have you done to him?"

"Hmmm, I know there's a shutoff here somewhere," said Sergeant Fish, fumbling with the weapon.

For a few minutes Eldon thought his head might explode. Everything he'd ever seen, heard, smelled, thought, tasted, and felt was crashing about his skull.

He felt the wet grass on his bare stomach when he was still a baby. He tasted sour milk, felt Henry Botkins's water balloon hit him in the fifth grade, heard a lion roaring at the circus. He felt a dog's wet tongue on his cheek. He saw Elvis sitting on a suitcase, crying. He saw forty movies in four seconds. He saw his father reaching down for him.

"Dad!"

Then everything went black.

18

AH-CHOO!

Through a dark haze Eldon could hear people shouting.

"Give him space to breathe!"

"He's coming around!"

"My son! What happened?"

"He's going to be all right, lady. Just give him some room."

Eldon's eyes fluttered open. He squinted up into a bank of bright lights and groaned. His neck hurt. Every muscle in his body felt as if it had been hammered.

"Sorry, kid," said Sergeant Fish. "You jumped right into the spot I was aiming at."

Eldon rubbed his eyes, groaned again, and sat up.

There was a ring of people around him. He recognized his mother, Annie, and Sergeant Fish.

The floor was cold and wet. He shook his head and tried to remember.

There had been a fight and an old man with a mop. He looked down and studied his lamé suit.

"Nothing to worry about anymore," said Sergeant Fish, leaning over. "The police are here. Those four won't be bothering you for a while."

"Huh?" said Eldon. He sniffled and wiped his nose with his arm. "What four?"

"Those fake Elvises," said the sergeant, pointing to Carl, Don, Burt, and John. "They were trying to ruin your career. Don't you remember?"

Eldon squinted. The four Presleys, their clothes soaked and torn, were standing, handcuffed, in front of the Fun Zone Arcade. Three policemen were close by, filling out reports.

"Don't you remember, son?" asked Mrs. Grant, kneeling down.

Eldon rubbed his sore neck. "I sort of do. I think."

"Do you remember me?" asked Annie, poking her head in his face.

Eldon nodded.

He sniffled again and wiped off his nose with his arm.

"What about me?" said Miss Abel, standing over him. She smiled. "Do you know who I am?"

Eldon squinted. "Are you my teacher?"

Miss Abel sighed.

"Kathy Abel is the mall manager," said Annie. "She's the one that promised the crowd you'd sing today."

"Sing?" said Eldon. He put a hand to his chest and gulped. "What do you mean sing?"

"Don't try to get out of it now," said Miss Abel. "I already have to tell them the imitators aren't coming. If you back out too, they'll go crazy. Just listen to them."

Eldon wrinkled his nose and cupped a hand to his ear. In the distance he could hear the crowd chanting. "Elvis or else! Elvis or else! Elvis or else!"

"There are twenty thousand people in the parking lot expecting to hear you sing," said Miss Abel. "If you don't go on, there's going to be a riot."

"Twenty thousand people! A riot?" said Eldon. "I ah ah AH-CHOO!" He sneezed onto the floor.

Miss Abel winced and stepped back.

"Eldon, get up off that wet floor," said Mrs. Grant. "You're getting a cold."

"Mom, I always have a cold," said Eldon, slowly getting to his feet. "Geez. I'm not a baby, you know."

"You look a mess," said Miss Abel, surveying Eldon's wet soapy suit. "But there's no time to change. The crowd out there won't wait much longer."

"Geez, I don't know," said Eldon.

"Listen to them," said Miss Abel. "Elvis or else. If you don't sing, they're going to rip up this mall. Maybe even the whole city."

"She's right. You have to go on," said Annie. "The whole tour depends on it. The Japanese have even sent over a TV crew."

"The Japanese? TV?" said Eldon. "Ah . . . ah . . . ah-choo!"

He sniffled and stuck a finger in his mouth. "Hey! Where's my retainer?"

"You spit it out at your last concert," said Annie. She looked into his eyes. "That electricity must have scrambled your brains."

Eldon shrugged.

Miss Abel narrowed her eyes. "Listen, I don't like making threats, but you promised. If you don't go out there right now, I'll sue—for millions."

"Millions?" said Eldon. "But I don't even have hundreds."

"Then I suggest you go out and sing," said Miss Abel.

Annie glanced nervously down the long hallway. The chants outside were growing louder by the second. "Eldon, you have to go," she said. "You promised."

"But . . . but what if I freeze up?"

"You're a pro," said Annie. "You're not going to freeze up." Then she took him by the elbow and steered him toward the parking lot, where twenty thousand screaming fans were waiting.

19

SHAME! SHAME! SHAME!

"Elvis or else!" the people chanted, clapping their hands along with the words. "Elvis or else! Elvis or else!"

Eldon shaded his eyes against the blazing sun. He was just starting to get what was going on. "These people are here to see *me*?"

"Relax. You're going to be fine," said Annie, pushing him through the crowd.

Miss Abel bounded onto the wooden stage. When she grabbed the microphone it sent out a blast of feedback. *Ska-reech!*

Half the crowd clamped their hands over their ears.

"Sorry," said Miss Abel. "But now that I have your attention I—"

"Where's Elvis?" someone demanded.

"Elvis or else!" shouted a woman up front.

Miss Abel raised her hand for quiet.

"Now just a minute. Give me a chance."

"We want to know where Elvis is!" yelled someone in the crowd. "You better have a good answer, lady!"

"I'll answer you with a question of my own," said Miss Abel. "Are you ready to *party*?"

"Yes!" replied twenty thousand voices.

"Then I guess you're ready to *rock*!"

"Yes!"

"And ready to *roll*!"

"Yes! yes! yes!"

Annie pushed Eldon up the stairs and onto the stage. He stumbled toward Miss Abel. Someone handed him an electric guitar, and the crowd roared.

Eldon shaded his eyes and looked out at the sea of waving arms and bodies.

Miss Abel gripped the microphone with one hand and raised a fist high into the air. "Back from the dead! Live on our stage! The greatest singer in the history of rock. The one! The only! King of rock and roll . . . ! It's Elll-viss!"

The crowd went crazy. The roar could be heard for miles. Eldon sniffled and stepped to the microphone as Miss Abel hurried offstage.

He gazed dumbly at the TV cameras, at the exploding flashbulbs, at the endless sea of people surging toward the stage, falling back, and surging forward again. Some people had fainted, others were crying. Still others seemed to be frozen in place, mouths open, staring blankly.

"Eldon!" screamed Annie from the side of the stage. " 'Hound Dog'!"

Eldon held onto the microphone as tightly as he could. He was sure he'd faint if he let go.

"Sing!" shouted Miss Abel.

But Eldon couldn't move. All he could do was stand there, staring out at the crowd.

The cheering went on for five minutes, maybe more. To Eldon it felt like five hours.

Eventually the crowd began to realize something was wrong. Eldon hadn't waved, hadn't spoken, hadn't moved a muscle.

The cheering began to die down. Finally it stopped completely and a hush fell over the crowd.

"What's wrong with him?" asked Miss Abel.

"Eldon, sing!" said Annie, climbing onto the stage. "There's a world tour at stake, a million dollars."

Eldon didn't even turn his head.

Then someone yelled. "Fake!"

"We've been tricked!" shouted a woman in the front, shaking her fist. "He's not Elvis."

Eldon stared out blankly as the shouts and insults poured in on him like rotten fruit.

"He probably lip synched to a tape!"

"*The National Whisper* just wanted to sell papers!"

"The Mayfair Mall just wanted the advertising!"

"They used that poor kid!"

"Shame! Shame! Shame! Shame!"

The chant swept the crowd. Miss Abel climbed back onto the stage. She shielded her face from the verbal stones being hurled by the crowd.

"What are we going to do?" she asked Annie.

"We're going to get Eldon out of here," said Annie. "You grab him under one arm, I'll get him under the other."

And the two of them carried him off the stage, stiff as a frozen fish.

It wasn't until they were back inside the mall and had set him on a bench that he finally moved.

"I told you I wasn't him," he mumbled, shaking his head. "Geez. That was terrible."

"A few hours ago you were him," said Annie. "One hundred percent."

"It must have been the taser shock," said Miss Abel. She glared at Sergeant Fish. "You drove Elvis away."

"He saved Eldon's life," said a white-haired

woman, suddenly stepping out from behind a potted palm. It was Miss Lilly. She placed a wrinkled hand on Eldon's forehead and shut her eyes. "Mr. Presley has departed. All that's left is Eldon Grant."

"Thank goodness," sighed Mrs. Grant.

"If it weren't for this gentleman here, Elvis would have eventually killed him. Believe me, this man's a hero."

Sergeant Fish grinned and polished his badge with his hand. "Just doing my duty, ma'm."

Miss Lilly patted Eldon on the cheek and smiled sweetly. "Take care now. I predict you're going to lead a long, eventful life, as yourself."

"Will I ever get to be a superstar?" asked Eldon. It had felt terrible standing in front of that huge crowd, but having friends at school was a different story. He was going to miss that part of being Elvis.

"You'll always be my superstar," Mrs. Grant chimed in. "When you disappeared, my heart just about broke."

Annie nodded. "So we won't be going to Japan," she said. "But I'm glad to have you back."

Eldon grinned at his friend. "Do me a favor and leave me out of your next newspaper article, all right?"

"The next story is already written," said Annie. "I've learned something terrible about the cafeteria." She lowered her voice. "Poisoned food."

"Spare me the gore." Eldon raised his hand. "I've already had enough excitement for the day."

"You've led two lives," said Miss Lilly. "Not many people can say that. You're pretty lucky, you know."

"Believe me. I know," said Eldon.

In fact, at that moment he felt like the luckiest kid on earth. For, if he hadn't fallen down earlier and soaked his clothes, everyone in the crowd would have known that while up onstage he'd peed in his pants.

20

HOME RUN

 That night Eldon's mother came upstairs and sat on the edge of his bed. The light of the full moon drifted through the leaves on the cottonwood outside, filling the room with shadowy butterflies.

"I'm so glad you're back," Mrs. Grant said. "For a while there I thought I'd lost you. I don't know what I would have done. First your father, then . . ." Her voice trailed off.

"It's all right, Mom," said Eldon. He turned toward the window and drank in the sweet smell of the warm spring evening. "I'm home now."

"It must have been horrible," said Eldon's mother.

"Horrible?" Eldon shook his head. "There were some things I didn't like very much, but for a little while I was the king of the world. I had everything, money, fame, girls . . ." Eldon swallowed, choking back a tear. "Mom, I couldn't tell you this before, but something fantastic happened too."

"Something fantastic?" said Mrs. Grant.

Eldon reached out and took his mother's hand. "Remember when Sergeant Fish shot me?"

"Of course."

"All kinds of things went through my head, memories mostly, but other things too."

"Other things?"

"I saw Elvis sitting on a suitcase, crying. The electricity was sending him away, but he didn't want to go."

"Who could blame him," said Eldon's mom.

"He said a man was waiting to see me, a man who'd made a difficult journey to be there."

"A man?" asked Mrs. Grant. Her lip quivered. "What man?"

"A man who'd come to deliver a message," said Eldon.

"What message?"

Eldon watched the shadow butterflies dance across his mother's face.

"What did he say?" asked Mrs. Grant.

Eldon looked down, then raised his head and softly

smiled. "All he said was 'Keep your eye on the ball, the weight on your back foot, and swing from the hips.' "

Mrs. Grant gasped. "Your father!"

Eldon bit his lip. "Mom, there was something else too."

Mrs. Grant's eyes glistened. "Something else?"

Eldon gave his mother a kiss. "Father said that was for you, with love."

Mrs. Grant shut her eyes and drank in the moment. Then she took a deep breath and let out a sigh she'd been holding in for years.

"I'm going to hit a homer, Mom."

Eldon's mom wrapped her arms around her son and squeezed him tight. "Oh, Eldon, you just did."

ELVIS PRESLEY WORD SEARCH

Can you find the following words and phrases in the word-search puzzle?

BLUE SUEDE SHOES   **CAPRICORN**
ED SULLIVAN SHOW   **GRACELAND**
GRITS   **GUITAR**
HOUND DOG   **JAILHOUSE ROCK**
MEMPHIS   **PINK CADILLAC**

```
S V W B D C A W P T E S H L V K
E D S U L L I V A N S H O W B R
L S I H P M E M S L K R U F C O
A V S C A L L I D A C K N I P T
N I I D M Y T E F L O M D N E I
T N H S R P U I A S R T D I B R
W R J H I R V T B D E O O B F A
O O P O C B W X G T S P G S H E
H C S E O H S E D E U S E U L B
S I R M I C R C M H O E T M I Y
J R A T N A E D O G H L A S A D
A P E D T D C B N M L G T C C D
I A V I A U M D S T I R G V I E
L C U B D N A L E C A R G T E T
G G E D C R B Z X A J O P L V E
T T A E J A I T P H A U S E T R
```

ABOUT THE AUTHOR

Stephen Mooser is the author of many books for young readers, including the Creepy Creature Club series. He lives in Bar Harbor, Maine.